RAHAB of Jericho

By
Constance Lee

authorHOUSE®

AuthorHouse™
1663 Liberty Drive
Bloomington, IN 47403
www.authorhouse.com
Phone: 1-800-839-8640

First published by AuthorHouse 2/23/2010

ISBN: 978-1-4490-4859-4 (e)
ISBN: 978-1-4490-4857-0 (sc)

Library of Congress Control Number: 2009912182

Printed in the United States of America
Bloomington, Indiana

This book is printed on acid-free paper.

This book is dedicated to:

Travis and Rashid

Preface

Apostle Paul wrote,

"Now faith is the substance of things hoped for, the evidence of things not seen. For by it the elders obtained a good report.

Through faith we understand that the worlds were framed by the word of God, so that things which are seen were not made of things which do appear.

But without faith, it is impossible to please him: for he that cometh to God must believe that he is, and that he is a rewarder of them that diligently seek him….

By faith the walls of Jericho fell down, after they were compassed about seven days.

By faith the harlot, <u>Rahab</u>, perished not with them that believed not, when she had received the spies with peace.

And what shall I say more?"

Penned about 68 AD

(Read: Hebrews 11:1-3, 30-32)

Rahab lived in a time when men did not want to worship the Living God. In order to understand her, we just cannot look at her profession as a harlot. We have to go far beyond Rahab's time to the beginning of creation.

Rahab was not the only sinner on the face of the earth; neither is she the last sinner! She happens to be one of the sinners that decided to do something about her condition.

Some important people of God came to visit the city of Jericho where Rahab lived. But these people were not ordinary people. They had strange customs. They served *One* God. Their God was powerful and did things that no other deity could do. In fact, their God *is* God!

Before we can talk about Rahab, we must understand the progression of mankind: sin; the flood; Noah; the God of Abraham, Isaac, and Jacob; Moses; Joshua; the children of Israel; their wilderness travels; the land of Canaan; then, the city of Jericho. Come and go with me…

Contents

Chapter One

Sin – Before & After the Flood

Life (on earth) is the same as before and after *the Flood*. We know that the **sons of God** *(fallen angels)* contributed to the multiplication and the downfall of the human race. Genesis 6:1-2, 4 states, ***"And it came to pass, when men began to multiply on the face of the earth, and daughters were born unto them, That the sons of God saw the daughters of men that they were fair; and they took them wives of all which they chose…There were giants in the earth in those days; and also after that** [REFERENCING THE DAYS OF ADAM AND NOAH], **when the sons of God came in unto the daughters of men, and they bare children to them, the same became mighty men which were of old, men of renown."***

Lucifer was there before creation, after re-creation (Genesis 1:3-2:25), [1] before the flood, and after the flood. Just because the waters of the flood receded off the face of the earth, it does not mean that the devil went away! *And today,* Satan is still here ***"seeking whom he may devour."*** (I Peter 5:8) In the day of his creation, Lucifer was made perfect *("the anointed cherub"),* [2] and God gave Lucifer dominion over the earth. But some where along the way, things changed for the worst. During the pre-*Adamite period,* Lucifer became *Satan* (i.e., the Devil: the great adversary of man and the captain of evil spirits and fallen angels). Lucifer got lifted up in pride, corrupted the pre-Adamites, slandered God, turned the hearts of the pre-Adamites against God, and lost his dominion over the earth. Then Lucifer went

---

[1]   When God created man, Satan was somewhere in the Garden of Eden hiding behind a bush.
[2]   ***"Thou wast perfect in thy ways from the day that thou wast created till iniquity was found in thee."*** (Read, Ezekiel 28:11-19)

stark "mad" and desired to ascend into the heavens: (1) to be like God; (2) to exalt his own throne above the stars of God; (3) to sit upon the mount of the congregation (the heavenly place of worship); (4) to ascend above the heights of the clouds; (5) to be like the most High. [3] Even worse, Lucifer rallied the other angels to help launch his campaign against God. After the war in heaven, Lucifer & Company (about one-third of heaven - rebelling angels) fell to the earth and destroyed it. As an eye witness, Jesus said, ***"I beheld Satan as lightning fall from heaven."*** (Luke 10:18)

Caption: Lucifer & Company fell as lightning from heaven.

---

[3]   Isaiah 14:12-15

So, God *re-created* the earth (including the sun, moon and the stars) and *created* a man in His image (Adam) to fellowship with Him. (Genesis 1:3-2:25) Happily, God gave Adam dominion over the earth. Next, God created a female chromosome from the DNA of one of Adam's ribs and made the most beautiful and perfect Wo-man in the earth. And Adam said, ***"This is now bone of my bones, and flesh of my flesh: she shall be called Woman, because she was taken out of Man. Therefore shall a man leave his father and his mother, and shall cleave unto his wife and they shall be one flesh."*** (Genesis 2:24) God sanctioned "marriage." He did not sanction *"the institution of shacking"* living together out of wedlock. Thus, God married "The Man" *to* "The Woman. [4] Also, God commissioned them to be ***"fruitful, multiply, and replenish the earth and subdue it."*** (Genesis 1:28) Lucifer was furious! It was Lucifer's plan to get back his control over the earth and he beguiled the Woman (through the serpent who spoke to her) to eat of the *"forbidden fruit"* ***(the tree of knowledge of god and evil)*** [5] in the Garden of Eden. Then, the Woman gave the "forbidden fruit" to Adam who *willingly* ate it.

In the cool of the day, God came down to the Garden of Eden looking for Adam and Eve. After holding court, God expelled Adam and Eve from the garden and He told the serpent, ***"Because thou hast done this, thou art cursed above all cattle, and above every beast of the field, upon thy belly shalt thou go, and dust shalt thou eat all the days of thy life. And I will put enmity between thee and the woman, and between thy seed and her seed; it shall bruise thy head, and thou shalt bruise his heel. Unto the woman he said, I will greatly multiply thy sorrow and thy conception; in sorrow thou shalt bring forth children; and thy desire shall be to thy husband, and he shall rules over thee. And unto Adam he said, Because thou hast hearkened unto the voice of thy wife, and hast eaten of the tree, of which I commanded thee, saying, Thou shalt not eat of it: cursed is the ground for thy sake; in sorrow shalt thou eat of it all the days of thy life. Thorns also and thistles shall it bring forth to thee; and thou shalt eat the herb of the field. In the sweat of thy face shalt thou eat bread, till thou return unto the ground; for out of it wast thou taken: for dust thou art, and unto dust shalt thou return."*** (Genesis 3:14-19)

---

[4]   God created and married two people of the opposite sex - male and female (not same sex marriages).
[5]   Genesis 2:16-17

Caption: Re-creation.

Caption: Re- creation – the earth restored.

After the court session was over, ***"Adam called his wife's name Eve because she was the mother of all living."*** (Genesis 3:20) Although Adam was extremely intelligent, he was stupid! Previous to the deception, Adam and Eve were sinless! Adam allowed Eve to entice him and Satan to deceive him. God gave Adam one strict command, ***"Do not eat of the tree of knowledge..."*** Therefore, God had no choice but to sentence and expel them from the Garden of Eden.

Before expulsion from heaven, Lucifer (once the most *magnificent cherub*) personally knew God the Father, the Son, and the Holy Ghost and he knew the no-tolerance rule to sin! Can you imagine, Lucifer walked and talked with God *face-to-face!* In spite of Lucifer's fellowship with the Godhead, *he still sinned!* Also, he knew the plan of salvation for the human race and he knew that God's plan existed before the creation of the earth. Do not be dismayed, *"**God is not mocked.**"* (Galatians 6:7) God knew that Lucifer would be lifted up in pride. In fact, any one of the lesser angels could have incited a rebellion in heaven. Thus, God had a backup plan.

Lucifer flew throughout the worlds and the universe looking for ways to destroy mankind. Finally, he launched a master plan through the human race (via Adam and Eve) and his personalized agents to destroy the prophecy regarding the "seed of the woman" ***(Jesus Christ, the Savior and the Anointed One).*** Lucifer's plan was executed through the intermarriages of the *daughters of men* to the *sons of God* ("fallen angels") - an army of supernatural beings expelled from heaven along with him. From this union, giants were born to the daughters of men and this race was created to *corrupt* the human race and to thwart the birth of Jesus. The lineage and the *bloodline* of Jesus' ancestors would have been tarnished with the *bloodline* of the fallen angels [6] who were not of this world. Furthermore, all of the fallen angels (including Lucifer) cannot be saved or redeemed by the blood of Jesus Christ. God's *plan of salvation* is only for the human race! [7] ***"God has chosen us in him before the foundation of the world to be holy and without blame... Predestined us unto adoption...Made us accepted...In whom we have redemption through his blood, the forgiveness of sins, according to the riches of his grace...He hath abounded toward us in all wisdom and prudence...Made known unto us the mystery of his will according to his good pleasure..."*** (Ephesians 1:4-9)

---

[6]   Fallen angels were not men, they were supernatural beings not of this world.
[7]   Read: I Peter 3:19; II Peter 2:4; and Jude 6-7.

Chapter Two

Noah – the Call

"**But Noah** [the only righteous man of all the living souls on the earth] **found GRACE in the eyes of the Lord…Noah was a just man and perfect in his generation and Noah walked with God…And God said unto Noah, The end of all flesh is come before me; for the earth is filled with violence through them; and, behold, I will destroy them with the earth.**" (Genesis 6:8-9, 12)

Noah's Deluge

"<u>And God saw that the wickedness of man was great in the earth and that every imagination of the thoughts of his heart was only evil continually. And it repented the Lord that he had made man on the earth, and it grieved him at his heart. And the Lord said, I will destroy man whom I have created from the face of the earth: both man, and beast, and the creeping thing, and the fowls of the air; for it repenteth me that I have made them… The earth was filled with violence. And God looked upon the earth, and, behold, it was corrupt; for all flesh had corrupted his way upon the earth.</u>" (Genesis 6:5-7, 11-12)

"*Make thee an ark of gopher wood; rooms shalt thou make in the ark, and shalt pit it within and without with pitch. And this is the fashion which thou shalt make it of: The length of the ark shall be three hundred cubits, the breadth of it fifty cubits, and the height of it thirty cubits. A window shalt thou make to the ark, and in a cub it shalt thou finish it above; and the door of the ark shalt thou set in the side thereof; with lower second, and third stories shalt thou make it.*[8] *And, behold, I even I, do bring a flood of waters upon the earth, to destroy all flesh, wherein is the breath of life, from under heaven; and every thing that is in the earth shall die."* (Genesis 6:14-17)

"But with thee will I establish my covenant; and thou shalt come into the ark, thou and thy sons, and thy wife, and thy sons' wives with thee. And of every living thing of all flesh, two of every sort shalt thou bring into the ark, to keep them alive with thee; they shall be male and female. Of fowls after their kind, and of cattle after their kind, of every creeping thing of the earth after his kind, two of every sort shall come unto thee to keep them alive. And take thou unto thee of all food that is eaten, and thou shalt gather it to thee; and it shall be for food for thee, and for them. Thus did Noah; according to all that God commanded him, so did he." (Genesis 6:18-22)

"And the Lord said unto Noah, <u>Come thou and all thy house into the ark</u>… Of every clean beast thou shalt take to thee by sevens, the male and his female: and of beasts that are not clean by two, the male and his female. Of fowls also of the air by sevens, the male and the female; to keep seed alive upon the face of all the earth." (Genesis 7:1-3)

"For yet seven days, and I will cause it to rain upon the earth forty days and forty nights; and every living substance that I have made will I destroy from off the face of the earth. And Noah did according unto all that the Lord commanded him." (Genesis 7:4-5)

God blessed the human race through *six* [9] souls, *"And God spake unto Noah, saying, Go forth of the ark, thou and thy wife, and thy sons, and thy sons' wives with thee…<u>And Noah built an altar unto the Lord</u> and took of every clean beast, and of every clean fowl, and offered burnt offerings on the altar. And the Lord smelled a sweet savour; and the Lord said in his heart, I will not again curse the ground any more for man's sake; for the imagination of man's heart is evil from his youth; neither will I again smite any more every thing*

---

[8]   It has been said that a cubit is 25 inches; so the ark was about 625 ft. in length; 104 ft. in width; and 62-½ ft. in height. There was a window for light on all three stories of the ark.

[9]   Noah only had three sons and each one of them had one wife.

living, as I have done. While the earth remaineth, seedtime and harvest, and cold and heat, and summer and winter, and day and night shall not cease…" (Genesis 8:16, 20-22)

Genesis 9:1, 19-20 states, *"And God blessed Noah and his sons, <u>and said unto them, Be fruitful, and multiply, and replenish the earth</u>…And the sons of Noah that went forth of the ark were Shem, Ham, and Japheth. These are the three sons on Noah and of them was the whole earth overspread."*

"Noah was five hundred (500) years old when he begat Shem, Ham, and Japheth." (Genesis 5:32) About 2348 BC, the following is true of the flood: *Noah* was six hundred (600) years old entering the ark (Genesis 7:11); *Japheth* was one hundred (100) years old; *Shem* was ninety-eight [10] (98) years old; and *Ham* was about ninety-seven (97) years old. Noah's sons (Shem, Ham and Japheth) did not have offspring until after the flood. (Genesis 21:5)

We do not know what Noah, Shem, Ham, Japheth and their wives looked like (i.e., facial structures, eye shape and color, hair type such as wavy, kinky, curly, or straight, skin type such as pale, light, dark but assuredly weather beaten, weight, or height). But one thing we do know is that every race, color, shape and size of men came from *the sons of Noah*. [11] Certainly, they must have been mentally, spiritually, and physically fit in light of the monumental task assigned to them. Surely, they ate natural and wholesome foods, so they had healthy diets. They worked outdoors everyday for one hundred and twenty years (120) building the ark, so they got a great deal of bodily exercise. In addition, we must give them credit for gathering all of the materials, grains, straw, hay, water, food, vessels, building stalls for the ark's occupants, and escorting the animals that God spoke into their minds to cooperate with Noah & Company.

Regardless of their ages, we can assume that *Noah's sons* (Shem, Ham, and Japheth) thoroughly enjoyed "sex" with their wives and that their levels of testosterone was

---

[10]   Two years after the flood, Shem was 100 yrs old when he begat Arphaxad. Perhaps, his wife gave birth to daughters. (Genesis 11:10)

[11]   Genesis 10:1-32 (the generations of Noah's sons); Genesis 25:12-16 (Ishmael's sons; Genesis 25:1-34 (Abraham & Keturah's sons); and Genesis 36:1-43 (Esau's sons).

quite high; but, they were doing *exactly as* God commissioned them *to replenish the earth.* Also, we must give credit to their wives who submitted themselves to their husbands, because God commissioned them as well. Furthermore, we must give God **"all the glory"** because He gave Shem, Ham, and Japheth the mindset and the stamina to complete such a horrendous task. Any one else, would have said, "Lord, Are you crazy? Six people cannot replenish the earth!" But, God would have said, "Have you considered my servants *Adam and Eve?* Case closed!"

Mankind's Life Span Shortened

In Scripture, God shorten man's life span about two times: (1) Genesis 6:3 states, **"The Lord said, My spirit shall not always strive with man, for that he also is flesh: yet his days shall be an hundred and twenty years."** Prior to this, Adam (like many others) lived past nine hundred years. Adam lived to be 930 years. (Genesis 5:5) (2) Psalm 90:10 states, **"The days of our years are threescore years and ten [70 years]; and if by reason of strength they be fourscore years [80 years], <u>yet is their strength labor and sorrow; for it is soon cut off, and we fly away.</u>"** Modern men fall under the Psalm 90:10 lifespan, and for the most part, he is lazy. Today, most people suffer from chronic illnesses, bad diets, obesity, little bodily exercise, bowlegs, flat feet, and bad backs! Very rarely, people live to be one hundred years old. In contrast, Noah lived to be 950 years. (Genesis 9:29) But for 120 years, Noah constructed the ark as he preached "righteousness" to the heathens. Hypothetically, *if Noah were alive* (today) and should he asks three men (unrelated to him) to help him build a humongous ship for 120 years, they would laugh at him and lock him up in a "nut house" and throw away the key. Regarding man's life span, God penned one more mandate - **a disobedient child shall live one half of his days!**

Noah's Prophecy

After surviving the flood and seeing a beautiful bow of colors *(the rainbow)* in the sky as the seal of **"God's covenant with all flesh and every living creature upon the earth,"** Noah celebrated. (Genesis 9:13-21) Like any one else having experienced *a catastrophic ordeal* (the whole human race and every living creature destroyed before one's eyes), **Noah got drunk!** So, Noah became a husbandman, planted a vineyard, and said, *"Yippy!"* While asleep, his younger son (Ham) *looked upon his father's nakedness* and told his brothers, **"And Shem and Japheth took a garment, and laid it upon both their shoulders, and went backward, and covered the nakedness of their father; and their faces were backward, and they saw not their father's nakedness. And Noah awoke from his wine, and he knew that his younger son had done unto him. And he said, <u>Blessed be the Lord God of Shem; and Canaan shall be his servant. God shall enlarge Japheth, and he shall dwell in the tents of Shem; and Canaan shall be his servant</u>."** (Genesis 9:24-26)

God is sovereign and He can do whatever, whenever, and however He pleases. Surely, death and life are in the tongue. (Proverbs 18:21) Through *Noah's tongue,* prophecies went forth: (1) Noah forecasted Shem's race as the "chosen race" and he *hallowed* the **Lord God** of Shem; (2) Noah blessed Japheth with *"enlargement;"* and (3) Noah cursed Ham *"with servitude"* to Shem and Japheth. So, God looked down from heaven and decided that He would take the "land of Canaan" from Ham's posterity and give it to Shem's posterity.

One Language

By Genesis 11:1, **"...<u>the whole earth was of one language [Hebrew] and of one speech</u>."**

In Genesis 11:2-9, just one hundred years after the flood, human government fell flat on its face, **"And the Lord came down to see the city and the tower which the children of men built. And the Lord said, Behold the people is one and they have all one language: and this they begin to do; and now nothing will be restrained from them, which they have imagined to do. Go to, let us go down, and there confound their language, that they may not understand one another's speech. So the Lord scattered them abroad from thence upon the face of all the earth: and they left off to build the city. <u>Therefore is the name of it called Babel; because the Lord did there confound the language of all the earth:</u> and from thence did the Lord scatter them abroad upon the face of all the earth."**

Abraham - the Call

"Now the Lord said unto Abraham, Get thee out of thy country, and from thy kindred and from thy father's house, unto a land that I will shew thee..." (Genesis12:1)

Abraham obeyed God. By Genesis 13:12, *"Abram dwelt in the land of Canaan."* So, God told Abraham (who was dwelling in the land of Canaan), *"Arise, walk through the land [Canaan] in the length of it and in the breadth of it; for I will give it unto thee. Then Abram removed his tent, and came and dwelt in the plain of Mamre, which is in Hebron, and built there an altar unto the Lord... my covenant is with thee, and thou shalt be a father of many nations...And I will make thee exceeding fruitful, and I will make nations of thee, and kings shall come out of thee. And I will establish my covenant between me and thee and thy seed after thee in their generations for an everlasting covenant, to be a God unto thee, and to thy seed after thee. And I will give unto thee, and to thy seed after thee, the land wherein thou art a stranger, <u>all the land of Canaan</u>, for an everlasting possession; and I will be their God."* (Genesis 13:17-18; 17:4, 6-8)

God told Abraham, *"Look now toward heaven, and tell the stars, if thou be able to number them: and he said unto him, so shall thy seed be. And he believed in the Lord and he counted it to him for righteousness."* (Genesis 15:5-8) However, there is a down side to this. Unfortunately, God revealed a horrible prophecy concerning Abraham's posterity, *<u>"Know of surety that thy seed shall be a stranger in a land that is not theirs and shall serve them; and they shall afflict them four hundred years.</u> And also that nation, whom they shall serve, will I judge; and afterward shall they come out with great substance. And thou shalt go to thy father in peace; thou shalt be buried in a good old age. But in the fourth generation, <u>they shall come hither again</u> for the iniquity of the Amorites is not yet full."* In other words, God told Abraham that I am going to place your descendants in a strange place under servitude; but I shall remember them and bring them back to the land on which I promised you - *after 400 years.* In the meantime, God said that he would give the Canaanites *all the room they needed* to fulfill their sinful natures. Then, God planned to *"lower the boom"* on them.

Truly, there is nothing impossible for the Lord to do. (Genesis 18:14) Miraculously, Sarah (the wife of Abraham) was ninety (90) years old and past the age of childbearing when Isaac (means *"laughter"*) was born. (Genesis 17:19) And from this, we can conclude as the Bible states, ***"Therefore, Sarah laughed within herself, saying, <u>Shall I have pleasure</u>, my lord [Abraham] being old."*** (Genesis 18:13) Perhaps, Abraham and Sarah were ***"old and well stricken in age,"*** but they still enjoyed one another's company.

God promised Abraham, Isaac, and Jacob (including all of their descendants) greatness in numbers. Not only did they have high levels of testosterones but they enjoyed sex, ***"And I will make thy seed as the dust of the earth: so that if a man can number the dust of the earth, then shall thy seed also be numbered...And He brought him forth abroad, and said, Look now toward heaven, and tell the stars, if thou be able to number them: and he said unto him, So shall thy seed be...And he believed in the Lord; and he counted it to him for righteousness."*** (Genesis 13:16; 15:5-6) Therefore, in order to multiply as the dust of the earth and as the stars of heaven, they had to have *"sex"* and it gave them much *"pleasure."*

Moses – the Call

Surely, God said within Himself, it is time for me to fulfill my promise to my servant, Abraham. I will *"free"* the Hebrew slaves, *"bring my people out with great substance,"* and *"judge"* the Egyptians. So, God decided to use a Hebrew male right under Pharaoh's nose in his court. This male baby was saved from Pharaoh's edict ***"to cast every son that is born unto the Hebrews into the river."*** (Exodus 1:22) At first Pharaoh told the Hebrew midwives to destroy all the Hebrew male children after birth, but the midwives feared God and saved the baby boys. Many babies were murdered and many were put aside. There was one baby boy whose parents hid him and finally the mother placed him in an ark of bulrushes and *put him on the Nile River.* Ironically, the daughter of Pharaoh (the Hebrews' number one enemy) *rescued* this baby boy and *named* him, *"Moses"* (means *"drawn out"*). Moreover, Pharaoh's daughter paid Moses' mother (Jochebed) to nurse him. Isn't that just like the Lord, He used the father and the daughter to save the life of his servant, Moses. Now as a grown man, Moses' resume included an education as a prince of Egypt, experience in the desert, and a shepherd of sheep. God selected Moses who was obedient, meek, and a humble man [12] to lead His chosen people to the Promised Land.

Moses was on the backside of the desert when he came to the mountain of God, *Horeb.* He was attending the flock of Jethro (a shepherd and priest by profession, and Moses' father in law). Something quite spectacular happened to Moses, ***"The angel of the Lord appeared unto him in a flame of fire out of the midst of a burning bush but the bush was not consumed. And Moses said, I will turn aside and see this great sight…And when the Lord saw that he turned aside to see, God called unto him out of the midst of the bush, and said, Moses, Moses. And he said, Here am I. And he said Draw not nigh hither: put off thy shoes from off thy feet, for the place whereon thou standest is holy ground. Moreover, he said, I am the God of thy father, the God of Abraham, the God of Isaac, and the God of Jacob. And Moses hid his face; for he was afraid to look upon God. And the Lord said, I have surely seen the affliction of my people which are in Egypt, and have heard their cry by reason of their taskmasters; for I know their sorrows; <u>And I am come down to deliver them out of the hand of the Egyptians, and to bring them up out of that land unto a good land and a large, unto a land flowing with milk and honey; unto the place of the Canaanites, the Hittites, the Amorites, the Perizzites, the Hivites, and the Jebusites</u>…come now therefore, and <u>I will send thee unto Pharaoh that thou mayest bring forth my people the children of Israel out of Egypt.</u>"***

However, the cost of this privilege was very high. According to Hebrews 11:24-29 states, ***"By faith, Moses when he was come to years, <u>refused</u> to be called son of Pharaoh's daughter; Choosing rather to suffer affliction with the people of God than to enjoy the pleasures of sin for a season; Esteeming the reproach of Christ greater riches than the treasures of Egypt: for he had respect unto the recompence of the reward. By faith, he forsook Egypt not fearing the wrath of the king: for he endured, as seeing him is invisible. Through faith, he kept the Passover, and the sprinkling of blood, lest he that destroyed the firstborn should***

---

[12]   Numbers 12:3

touch them. By faith, they passed through the Red sea as by dry land: which the Egyptians assaying to do were drowned.”

Some unbelievers say that Moses was insane because: he killed an Egyptian to save a worthless Hebrew slave; he deserted the best *inn* in town with plenty of water, food, and drink (Pharaoh’s palace); he ran away to a dried-up desert without any protection or paid escorts; he married a poor Midianite desert girl; he became a penniless dirt shepherd; he went from riches to rags; he ruined his lucrative career in Egypt; he forfeited his chance to marry an Egyptian princess; he talked to a burning push; he turned stark gray after losing his mind; his face glowed as if he had been contaminated with radium; he made himself the leader over the Hebrew slaves; and he promised to deliver the Hebrew slaves without the use of weapons. In fact, Moses didn’t even *own* a slingshot.

Remarkably, the Bible states, *“For the wisdom of this world is foolishness with God. For it is written He taketh the wise in their own craftiness. And again, the Lord knoweth the thoughts of the wise that they are vain. Therefore, let no man glory in men.”* (I Corinthians 3:19-21) Thus Moses was not insane and God magnified Moses before the children of Israel, the Egyptians, and the world, *“Nevertheless, he [God] saved them for his name’s sake, that he might make his mighty power to be known. He rebuked the Red Sea also, and it was dried up: so he led them through the depth, as through the wilderness. And he saved them from the hand of him [Pharaoh] that hated them and redeemed them from the hand of the enemy.”* (Psalm 106:8-10)

Joshua - the Call

God remembered His promise to Abraham. When the iniquity of the Amorites (Canaanites) is fulfilled, His chosen people will return to the land of Canaan. After Moses’ death, *“The Lord spoke unto Joshua the son of Nun Moses’ minister saying, Arise, go over this Jordan, thou and all this people unto the land which I do give to them, even to the children of Israel. Every place that the sole of your foot shall tread upon that have I given unto you, as I said unto Moses... <u>There shall not any man be able to stand before thee all the days of thy life: as</u>*

I was with Moses, so I will be with thee: I will not fail thee, nor forsake thee. Be strong and of a good courage: for unto this people shalt thou divide for an inheritance the land which I sware unto their fathers to give them....do according to all the law which Moses my servant commanded thee: turn not from it to the right hand or to the left, that thou mayest prosper whithersoever thou goest." (Joshua 1:1-7)

However, only one thing changed – God was with Joshua (like Moses) but *He would no longer be in the midst of His people.* In Exodus 33:1-3, **"God told Moses that I will send an angel before them and drive out the Canaanite, Amorite, Hittite, Perizzite, Hivite, and the Jebusite. Unto a land flowing with milk and honey: for I will not go up in the midst of thee; for thou art a stiff-necked people; lest I consume thee in the way."**

This time, God did not want to destroy the entire earth. Instead, He ordered the children of Israel to destroy the Canaanites, **"And the Lord spake unto Moses in the plains of Moab by Jordan near Jericho, saying, Speak unto the children of Israel, and say unto them, When ye are passed over Jordan into the land of Canaan: Then ye shall drive out all the inhabitants of the land from before you, and destroy all their pictures [pornography], and destroy all their molten images [false gods], and quite pluck down all their high places; And ye shall dispossess the inhabitants of the land and dwell therein: for I have given you the land to possess it. And ye shall divide the land by lot for an inheritance among your families: and to the more ye shall give the more inheritance, and to the fewer ye shall give the less inheritance...But if ye will not drive out the inhabitants of the land from before you; then it shall come to pass, that those which ye let remain of them shall be pricks in your eyes, and thorns in your sides, and shall vex you in the land where ye dwell. Moreover it shall come to pass, that I shall do unto you as I thought to do unto them."** (Numbers 33:50-56)

Caption: *"And Noah built an altar unto the Lord…offered burnt offerings on the altar… And the Lord smelled a sweet savour…"* (Genesis 8:20-21)

Caption: Moses.

Caption: The Red Sea.

Chapter Three

The Promised Land, Canaan

Canaan is the *ancient* name for modern day Palestine. Canaan ("The Promised Land") covers a vast region with many, many, many settlements of migrant tribes. The ancient term, Biblical Canaanites, does not refer to a specific *ethnic* group, because the land of Canaan was filled with people from many nations. After the flood, all of these tribes are descendants of Noah's sons in one. Therefore, they are all inter-related as brothers.

Canaan's Ancient Borders

According to the Bible, the land of Canaan covers a vast area, *"And the border of the Canaanites was from Sidon, as thou comest to Gerar, unto Gaza; as thou goest, unto Sodom, and Gomorrah, and Admah, and Zeboim, even unto Lasha. These are the sons of Ham, after their families, after their tongues in their countries, and in their nations..."* (Genesis 10:19-20)

Southern Border - a total of about 81 miles or less:

"And the Lord spake unto Moses [a.k.a., Moshe Rabbeinu in Hebrew], saying, Command the children of Israel, and say unto them, When ye come into the land of Canaan; (this is the land that shall fall unto you for an inheritance, even the land of Canaan with the coasts thereof:) Then your south quarter shall be from the wilderness of Zin along by the coast of Edom and your south border shall be the outmost coast of the salt seas eastward: And your border shall turn

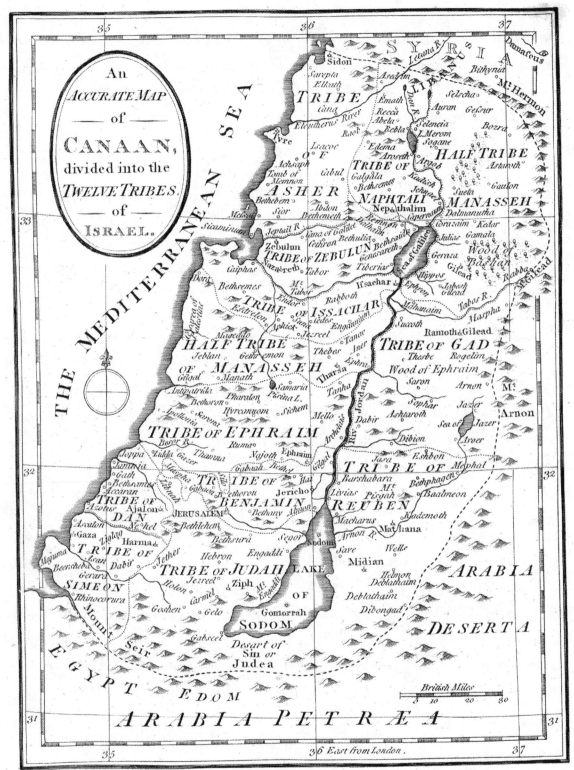

Caption: Map of Canaan

from the south to the ascent of Akrabbim [means "scorpions"], and pass on to Zin [a wilderness]: and the going forth thereof shall be from the south Kadesh-barnea [consecrated], and shall go on to Hazaraddar [village of Adar], and pass on to Azmon: And the border shall fetch a compass from Azmon unto the river of Egypt, and the goings out of it shall be at the sea." (Numbers 34:2-5)

<u>Western Border - a total of about 301 miles or less:</u>

"And as for the western border, ye shall even have the great sea for a border: this shall be your west border." (Numbers 34:6)

<u>Northern Border - a total of about 71 miles or less:</u>

"And this shall be your north border: from the great sea ye shall point out for you mount Hor ["the mountain"]: From mount Hor ye shall point out your border unto the entrance of Hamath ["fortress"]; and the goings forth of the border shall be to Zedad [unknown]: And the border shall go on to Ziphron [unknown], and the goings out of it shall be at Hazarenan ["village of fountains"]: this shall be your north border." (Numbers 34:7-9)

<u>Eastern Border - a total of about 280 miles or less:</u>

"And ye shall point out your east border from Hazarenan to Shepham: And the coast shall go down from Shepham to Riblah ["to increase or to multiply"], on the wast side of Ain ["eye"]; and the border shall descend, and shall reach unto the side of the sea of Chinnereth ["harp-shaped"] eastward: And the border shall go down to Jordan, and the goings out of it shall be at the salt sea: this shall be your land with the coasts thereof round about." (Numbers 34:10-12)

Problem - The Land Grant

Today, the question is who has right-of-way to *"The Land Grant"* for Palestine (ancient Canaan)? The answer is found in the Bible – **God's covenants with His chosen people.** Looking back at the Old Testament, the problem began with Abraham who put himself in a precarious position. He followed the wrong advice. He listened to Sarah (*emotionally distraught being childless)* who gave her handmaiden (Hagar, *"the bondwoman"*) to Abraham **"to obtain children by her."** (Genesis 16:2) So, Sarah thought God needed her help to "make things happen." Instead, she complicated God's plan. However, Abraham should have rejected Sarah's silly advice. Furthermore, Abraham should have said, **"Shut up!"** The Lord *don't* n-e-e-e-d your help, Sarai (Sarah)!" Being manly, Abraham's *testosterone* was "quite high" that day, he looked over at lovely Hagar, and he *willingly* obeyed Sarah's directives. However, if the wife was barren, it was customary procedure for the husband to obtain children by a concubine.

After Hagar conceived, she became conceited *(being emotionally overwhelmed that she was carrying Abraham's seed)* and despised her mistress, Sarah. This made Sarah very angry and she dealt harshly with Hagar. Well, what did Sarah expect? She *told* her husband to sleep with another woman! So, Hagar got mad and ran away to the wilderness by the fountain of Shur. It was there that the angel of the Lord [13] found her and made the *"Hagaric Covenant,"* [14] saying, **"Hagar, Sarai's maid** [NOT THE WIFE OF ABRAHAM] **whence camest thou? And whither wilt thou go? And she said, I flee from the face of my mistress Sarai. And the angel of the Lord said unto her, <u>Return to thy mistress and submit thyself under her hands</u>…I will multiply thy seed exceedingly, that it shall not be numbered for multitude. And the angel of the Lord said unto her, Behold thou art with child, and shalt bear a son and shalt call his name Ishmael: because the Lord hath healed thy affliction. And he will be a wild man; his hand will be against every man, and every man's hand against him; <u>and he shall dwell in the presence of all his brethren</u>. And she called the name of the Lord that spake unto her, Thou God seest me: for she said, Have**

---

[13]   In Scripture, the **"Angel of the Lord"** is the visible appearance or Theophany of the Lord Himself.
[14]   Hagaric Covenant: Genesis 16:7-14; 17:20; 21:17; 25:12

I also here looked after him that seeth me? Wherefore the well was called Beer-la-hai-roi; behold it is between Kadesh and Bered." (Genesis 16:7-14)

Caption: Abraham with his wife (Sarah), mistress, and sons.

Thus, Hagar returned to her mistress (Sarah) and gave birth to a healthy baby boy named *Ishmael* (means *"whom God hears"*). By the age of thirteen, Ishmael had a baby brother named *Isaac* (born unto Sarah and Abraham) but Ishmael *mocked* his little brother. Sarah picked-up on this jealously and ordered Abraham to send the bondwoman and her son (Hagar and Ishmael) away into the wilderness. Reluctantly, Abraham sent them away.

Frankly, God's word (concerning both brothers Isaac and Ishmael) is currently being fulfilled. The synopsis is simple: *"A man (Abraham)had two sons by two different women* and *after the death of the man each sons' descendants came forth to claim their birthright:"*

(1) The eldest son's descendants contend that **_Mother Hagar_** (a *bondwoman* and an Egyptian) was a concubine to their father (Abraham); Ishmael (as the eldest son) has full birthrights to his father's property and inheritance; he was circumcised at 13 years of age (according to God's covenant of circumcision with Abraham); his life was saved by Divine intervention; his *conception* was not prophesized by the Lord; the Lord Himself prophesized his name, destiny, and posterity to his mother; the Lord said that God will multiply his seed without number; **_BUT HE WILL DWELL IN THE PRESENCE OF ALL HIS BRETHREN_** [15]; he is the progenitor of twelve (12) princes and one daughter (Genesis 25:12-16); he is the father of nations; he would have to fight for his rights because every man's hand is against him; his descendants will be a great people; the bloodline is strengthened *between* Esau (Jacob's *twin brother*) and Ishmael due to Mahalath's [16] (a daughter of Ishmael) marriage to Esau; birthrights are politically strengthened; and finally, Ishmael *did not* want to leave his father, he was *forced* to leave because of Abraham's jealous wife, Sarah.

(2) The second son's descendants contend that **_Mother Sarah_** (a *free woman* and the half-sister to Abraham [17]) was the *first* wife to their father (Abraham); Sarah was from Haran (like Abraham) and she traveled with Abraham to the

---

[15]   Genesis 16:9-14

[16]   Ishmael's daughter Mahalath's (means *"sickness"*) name was changed to Basemath (means *"fragrance"*) was married to Esau (Jacob's twin brother). (Genesis 28:9; 36:3)

[17]   Genesis 20:12 Abraham and Sarah have the same father but not the same mother.

"land of Canaan;" Isaac is the only *full-blooded* offspring and he has *full* legal birthrights to all of his father's property and inheritance without dispute; **his conception was prophesized by the Lord Himself** [18] who came to visit his father on a hot summery day; he was circumcised approximately eight (8) days after birth (in accordance to God's covenant of circumcision); Abraham was circumcised at ninety-nine years of age; God renewed the Abrahamic Covenant with his son (Isaac, and his son, Jacob); there was no mention of Ishmael's name in that covenant; the promises of the Abrahamic Covenant passed on through his seed and his descendants as an everlasting covenant; their seed will be multiplied as "*the dust of the earth and the stars of the heavens;*" God <u>did not</u> make a covenant with Ishmael, instead, God made a covenant with his mother (Hagar) because He had *"pity"* [19] on her; God *"blessed"* Ishmael but said he will be ***"a wild man, against everyone and everyone will be against him, and <u>he will dwell in the presence of all his brethren.</u>"*** [20] And finally, after Sarah's death and Isaac's marriage to Rebecca, Abraham took a *second* wife *(Keturah)* who gave him six (6) more sons. [21] But, Abraham did not "bless" Keturah's sons, ***"<u>he gave them gifts and he sent them away east of Canaan from his son, Isaac.</u>"*** In fact, Abraham treated Keturah's sons in the same manner he did Hagar's son, Ishmael. Unlike Ishmael's descendants, none of Keturah's sons came forth to claim birthrights as descendants of Abraham. They were content with their gifts because ***"Abraham was rich in cattle, in silver, and in gold..."*** (Genesis 13:2) However, Abraham did not send Isaac away; instead, ***"<u>he gave all that he had to Isaac.</u>"*** (Genesis 25:5) On record, Isaac is the *second* son (in light of Ishmael and Keturah's six sons), but he is ***<u>the only</u>*** son to receive full-inheritance rights and privileges of the Abrahamic Covenant that he passed on to his son, ***Jacob.***

The Antidote - the Abrahamic and Sarahic Covenants

God has the final say regarding who gets what! Furthermore, the answer is found in the *Abrahamic and Sarahic Covenants.*

---

[18] Genesis 18:10 in the plans of Mamre.
[19] ***"...because the Lord hath heard thy affliction."*** (Genesis 17:11)
[20] Genesis 25:1-4; 25:18; 37:28; Judges 8:22-24)
[21] Genesis: 25:1-4 (List the nations and descendants of Abraham & Keturah)

<u>Abrahamic Covenant</u>

The Abrahamic Covenant was first before the Sarahic Covenant. ***"Now the Lord had said unto Abram, Get thee out of thy country, and from thy kindred, and from thy father's house, unto a land that I will shew thee. And I will make of thee a great nation, and I will bless thee, and make thy name great, and thou shalt be a blessing. And I will bless them that bless thee, and curse him that curseth thee: and in thee shall all families of the earth be blessed."*** (Genesis 12:1-3) At the age of seventy-five years old, Abram packed his bags and left with Sarai and Lot (his brother's son) for his *first sojourn* into Canaan, ***"And Abram passed through the land unto the place of Sichem, unto the plain of Moreh. And the Canaanite was then in the land."*** (Genesis 12:6) Then, God physically appeared to Abram, ***"And the Lord <u>appeared</u> unto Abram, and said, Unto thy seed will I give this land: and there built he an altar unto the Lord, who appeared unto him…and called upon the name of the Lord."*** (Genesis 12:7) [22] Then, God "enlarged" the Abrahamic Covenant as follows: ***"…the word of the Lord came unto Abram in a vision…Fear not I am thy shield and thy exceeding great reward… Look now toward heaven and tell the stars if thou be able to number them and so shall thy seed be…I brought thee out of the Chaldees to give thee this land to inherit it…In the same day the Lord made a covenant with Abram saying, Unto thy seed have I given this land, from the river of Egypt unto the great river, the river Euphrates…"*** (Genesis 15:1-21) By Genesis 17, God gave Abram a new name, ***"Abram fell on his face and God talked with him, saying, As for me, behold my covenant is with thee, and thou shalt be a father of many nations. Neither shall thy name any more be called Abram, <u>but thy name shall be Abraham;</u> for a father of many nations…I will make thee exceeding fruitful… make nations…kings shall come out of thee.. I will establish my covenant between me and thee and thy seed after thee in their generations for an everlasting covenant…and I will be their God."***

---

[22]   God made other appearances (in person, visions, and revelations) to Abraham. (Genesis 13:14; 15:1-21; 17:1-27; 18:1-33; 21:12; 22:1, 15)

Why did God give Canaan (the land flowing with milk and honey) to Abraham? Firstly, God loves the land of Canaan. Secondly, God told Moses, ***"For the land whether thou goest in to possess it, is not as the land of Egypt, from whence ye came out, where thou sowedst thy seed, and wateredst it with thy foot, as a garden of herbs: But the land whither ye go to possess it, is a land of hills and valleys, and drinketh water of the rain of heaven: A land which the Lord thy God careth for: the eyes of the Lord thy God are always upon it, from the beginning of the year even unto the end of the year.***" (Deuteronomy 11:10-12)

Sarahic Covenant

Before we talk about the Sarahic Covenant, let us examine Abraham's over-anxiousness for an heir. Considering Abraham's age, it is quite understandable why he wanted to *give away* the promise. Firstly, Sarah was *old* and *still* barren. Secondly, Abraham asked God to make his *personal* steward, Eliezer of Damascus, the *heir*. But, God said, ***"This shall not be thine heir; but he that shall come forth out of thine own bowels shall be thine heir.***" (Genesis 15:2-4) Thirdly, by Genesis 17:18, Abraham begged God, ***"O that Ishmael might live before thee."*** What did Abraham mean? Well, Abraham was about eighty six-years old and Sarah was *still* barren. So, Sarah gave her handmaid, Hagar, to Abraham and Ishmael was born. Without thinking, Abraham was crying out to God to make Ishmael his heir.

After God listened to Abraham's *whining*, He said, ***"As for Sarah thy wife, thou shalt not call her name Sarai, but Sarah shall her name be. And I will bless her, and give thee a son also of her: yea, I will bless her, and she shall be a mother of nations; kings of people shall be of her. Then Abraham fell upon his face, and laughed and said in his heart, Shall a child be born unto him that is an hundred years old? And shall Sarah that is ninety years old bear? And God [REPEATING HIMSELF A SECOND TIME] said, Sarah thy wife shall bear thee a son indeed; and thou shalt call his name, Isaac: and I will establish my covenant with him for an everlasting covenant, and with his seed after him."*** (Genesis 17:15-19)

By this time, God was *tired* of Abraham's *purring*. Then, God made reference to Abraham's son (Ishmael) saying, ***"As for Ishmael, <u>I have heard thee</u>: Behold, I have <u>BLESSED</u> him, and will make him fruitful, and will multiply him exceedingly; twelve princes shall he beget, and I will make him a great nation. <u>BUT MY COVENANT WILL I ESTABLISH WITH ISAAC</u> which Sarah shall bear unto thee at this time set time in the next year, And he left off talking with him, and God went up from Abraham."*** (Genesis 17:20-22)

Chapter Four

Table of Nations

In the Old Testament, the Book of Genesis 10:1-32 gives a complete list of the *"Table of Nations"*[23] beginning with Noah's three sons (Japheth, Ham, and Shem). For the purpose of this book, Ham and his decedents are the key players in the land of Canaan, but later they forfeited their rights to Shem and his descendants.

Ham - (His Descendants)

The Canaanites were the descendents of **Ham** (means *"hot"*), one of Noah's three sons. The Old Testament lists the Table of Nations for Ham, ***"And the sons of Ham; Cush, Mizarim, Phut, and Canaan...And Canaan begat Sidon, his firstborn, Heth [the progenitor of the Hittites], the Jebusite, the Amorite, the Girgasite, the Hivite, the Arkite, the Sinite, the Arvadite, the Zemarite, the Hamathite: and afterward were the families of the Canaanite spread abroad."*** (Genesis 10:6, 15-18) Ham's sons: **<u>Cush</u>,** [24] progenitor of various Ethiopian tribes who settled south of Egypt and they spread into: Arabia, Babylonia, India. (Genesis 10:6-12; I Chronicles 1:8-10; Isaiah 11:11); **<u>Mizraim</u>,** progenitor of various tribes upper and lower Egypt known as the land of Ham and the Philistines. (Genesis 10:6, 13-14; I Chronicles 1:8-11; Psalm 78:51; 105:23-27; 106:22); **<u>Phut</u>,** progenitor of Libyans and other northern tribes in Africa. (Genesis 10:6; Ezekiel 27:10; 35:5; 38:5; Jeremiah 46:9; Nahum 3:9); **<u>Canaan</u>,** progenitor of all the people who settled in Palestine, Arabia, Tyre, Sidon,

---

23   Read Genesis 10:1-32 for a list of the Table of Nations.
24   Cush begat Nimrod (a mighty hunter before the Lord) who founded Babel (Babylon), Erech, Accad, and Calneh in the land of Shinar. (Genesis 10:8-10)

including some of the land promised to Abraham. (Genesis 10:6, 15-19; 9:18-27; 15:18-21; I Chronicles 1:8-13; Deuteronomy 7:1-3; Joshua 12:1-24)

Japheth - (His Descendants)

The descendants of *Japheth* (means *"widespreading"* - Europe) are:

Gomer, progenitor of the ancient Galatians, Phrygians, Gauls, Celts, Germans, French, Welsh, Irish, British, and other Anglo-Saxon races. (Genesis 10:2-3; I Chronicles 1:5-6); **Magog,** progenitor of the Scythians and Tartars, descendants of modern Russia. (Ezekiel 38:2; 39:6; Revelations 20:8) Also, the name Magog referred to the country of the north of the Caucasus Mountains between the Black and Caspian seas; **Madai,** progenitor of the ancient Medes, Persians, and Hindoos. (Genesis 10:2; I Chronicles 1:5); **Javan,** progenitor of the Greeks, Italians, Spaniards, Portuguese, and other nations through Elishah, Tarshish, Dodanim, Kittim, identified with Cyprus, and the Mediterranean coastline. (Isaiah 23:1, 12; 66:19; Ezekiel 27:6, 13, 19, Numbers 24:24; I Chronicles 1:7; Daniel 11:30); **Tubal,** progenitor of the Iberians, Georgians, Cappadocians, other Asiatic and European races. (Genesis 10:2; I Chronicles 1:15); **Meshech,** progenitor of **Muscovite** tribes of Russia. (Genesis 10:2; I Chronicles 1:5); and **Tiras,** progenitor Thracians and Etruscans. (Genesis 10:2; I Chronicles 1:5)

Shem - (His Descendants)

The descendants of *Shem* (means *"name"* or *"renown"*) are: **Elam,** progenitor of the Elamites of the Persian Gulf. (Genesis 10:22; 14:1, 9; Isaiah 11:11; 21:2; 22:6; Jeremiah 25:25; 49:34-39; Ezekiel 32:24; Daniel 8:2); **Assur,** progenitor of the Assyrians. (Genesis 10:11, 22; Numbers 24:22-24; Ezekiel 27:23; 32:32; Hosea 14:3); **Arphaxad,** progenitor of the Israelites, Arabians, Edomites, Moabites, Ammonites, Ishmaelites, Midianites, and other tribes of Asia. (Genesis 20:22; 11:10-32: 17:20: 25:1-18; 36:1-43); **Lud,** progenitor of the Lydians of Asia Minor, the Ludim of Chaldea, and Persia. (Genesis 10:22); and **Aram,** progenitor of Aramaeans, the Syrians. (Genesis 10:22).

Chapter Five

The Moab Ordeal

__"And the Lord said unto me [Moses], Distress not the Moabites, neither contend with them in battle: for I will not give thee of their land for a possession; because I have given Ar unto the children of Lot for a possession."__ [25] (Deuteronomy 2:9)

These hostile residents included the Moabites who were distantly related to the children of Israel. The Moabites were descendants of an unholy union between Lot (the son of Haran) and his oldest daughter. Haran was the youngest brother of Abraham who took Lot with him on his journey from Ur of the Chaldees.[26] God destroyed Sodom, Gomorrah, the cities of the plains, and Lot's wife (who disobeyed the angel's instructions, looked back at the burning cities, and became a pillar of salt). Lot's daughters got their father drunk and each one slept (on a different night) with their father to extend the human race. After the destruction of the surrounding cities, Lot's daughters thought that there were no other people left in the world except them.

The children of Israel experienced great battles and bloodshed during their arrival to the Promised Land. Their victory caused the deaths of many people who refused to allow Joshua and the children of Israel permission to cross their lands.

---

[25]   At this time, God gave Moab to Lot; but later on it was given to Israel. (Psalm 60:6-9; Isaiah 11:14; Jeremiah 48:47)

[26]   Genesis 11:26-27

Balaam's Attempts to Curse Israel

It is important to include the children of Israel's "ordeal with Balak and Balaam" to show just how far people will go to outwit and overthrow God's people. Balak spent a great deal of money, time, and manpower to fight against Israel. He paid thousands of dollars for animals (rams and bullocks) to sacrifice to idol gods upon idol altars. In addition, king Balak spent thousands of dollars on materials and workers to build dozens of altars for these sacrifices. In the end, all of this was useless because the God of the children of Israel was with His people.

According to Numbers 22:1, *"...the children of Israel set forward and pitched in the plains of Moab on this side Jordan by Jericho."* At that time, Joshua (means *"Jehovah is salvation"*) and the children of Israel had just defeated the *giant* Amorite kings, Og (king of Bashan) and Sihon (king of Hesbron), and they were camped east of the Jordan River. This battle was a great defeat for the Amorites because Joshua and the children of Israel conquered and possessed all the land (north of the Arnon River to Moab's borders) that set the stage for their next ordeal with king Balak of Moab. Balak (the son of Zippor) was afraid and jealous of the children of Israel and he sent his princes to hire Balaam (means *"which see,"* a spiritualist and/or diviner) to curse the children of Israel.

To make a long story short, Balaam tried three times to curse the children of Israel but instead he blessed them:

First Attempt*:* Balaam prepared seven new alters never used to worship any idol god. *"And God met Balaam and he said unto him, I have prepared seven altars, and I have offered upon every altar a bullock and a ram. And the Lord put a word in Balaam's mouth, and said, Return unto Balak, and thus thou shalt speak. And he returned unto him and, lo, he stood by his burnt sacrifice, he, and all the princes of Moab. And he took up his parable and said, Balak the king of Moab hath brought me from Aram, out of the mountains of the east, saying, come, curse me Jacob, and come, defy Israel. <u>How shall I curse, whom God hat not cursed? Or how shall I defy, whom the Lord hath not defied?</u> For from the top of the rocks I see him, and from the hills I behold him: <u>lo, the</u>*

people shall dwell alone, and shall not be reckoned among the nations. Who can count the dust of Jacob, and the number of the forth part of Israel? Let me die the death of the righteous and let my last end be like his. And Balak said unto Balaam, What hast thou done unto me? I took thee to curse mine enemies, and behold, thou hast blessed them altogether. And he [Balaam] answered and said, Must I not take heed to speak that which the Lord hath put in my mouth?" (Numbers 23:4-12)

Second Attempt: King Balak took Balaam to another location to curse the children of Israel. *"And Balak said unto him [Balaam] Come, I pray thee, with me unto another place, from whence thou mayest see them…and curse me them from thence…And he brought him into the field of Zophim [field of watchers, a high place], to the top of Pisgah [part of a rugged mountain chain, called the Abarim] and built seven altars, and offered a bullock and a ram on every altar. And he said unto Balak, Stand here by thy burnt offering, while I meet the Lord yonder. And the Lord met Balaam and put a word in his mouth, and said, Go again unto Balak and say thus. And when he came to him, behold, he stood by his burnt offering, and the princes of Moab with him. And Balak said unto him, What hath the Lord spoken? And he took up his parable, and said, Rise up, Balak and hear; hearken unto me thou son of Zippor: God is not a man that he should lie; neither the son of man that he should repent: hath he said, and shall he not do it? Or hath he spoken, and shall he not make it good? Behold, I have received commandment to bless: and he hath blessed; and I cannot reverse it. He hath not beheld iniquity in Jacob, neither hath he seen perverseness in Israel: the Lord his God is with him, and the shout of a king is among them. God brought them out of Egypt; he hath as it were the strength of an unicorn. Surely there is enchantment against Jacob, neither is there any divination against Israel: according to this time it shall be said of Jacob and of Israel, What hath God wrought. Behold, the people shall rise up as a great lion, and lift up himself as a young lion: he shall not lie down until he eat of the prey, and drink the blood of the slain. And Balak said unto Balaam, Neither curse them at all, nor bless them at all. But Balaam answered and said unto Balak, Told not I thee, saying, All that the Lord speaketh, that I must do?"* (Numbers 23:13-26)

Third Attempt: King Balak took Balaam to the third location to curse the children of Israel. *"And Balak said unto Balaam, come, I pray thee, I will bring thee unto another place; peradventure it will please God that thou mayest curse me them from thence. And Balak brought Balaam unto the top of Peor* [a mountain which means opening, cleft], *that looketh toward Jeshimon* [a wilderness]. *And Balaam said unto Balak, Build me here seven altars and prepare me here seven bullocks and seven rams. And Balak did as Balaam had said, and offered a bullock and a ram on every altar. And when Balaam saw that it pleased the Lord to bless Israel, he went not, as at other times, to seek for enchantments, but he set his face toward the wilderness. And Balaam lifted up his eyes, and he saw Israel abiding in his tents according to their tribes; and the spirit of God came upon him. And he took up his parable, and said Balaam the son of Beor hath said, and the man who eyes are open hath said: He hath said, which heard the words of God, which saw the vision of the Almighty falling into a trance, but having his eyes open: How goodly are thy tents, O Jacob, and thy tabernacles, O Israel. As the valleys are thy spread forth, as gardens by the river's side, as the trees of lign* [wood] *aloes which the Lord hath planted, and as cedar trees beside waters. He shall pour the water out of his buckets, and his seed shall be in many waters, and his king shall be higher than Agag, and his kingdom shall be exalted. God brought him forth out of Egypt; he hath as it were the strength of a unicorn: he shall eat up the nations his enemies, and shall break their bones, and pierce them through with his arrows. He couched, he lay down as a lion, and as a great lion: who shall stir him up? Blessed is he that blesseth thee, and cursed is he that curseth thee. And Balak's anger was kindled against Balaam, and he smote his hands together and Balak said unto Balaam, I called thee to curse mine enemies, and, behold, thou has altogether blessed them these three times. Therefore, now flee thou to thy place: I thought to promote thee unto great honour; but, lo, the Lord hath kept thee back from honor. And Balaam said unto Balak, Spake I not also to thy messengers which thou sentest unto me, saying, If Balak would give me his house full of silver and gold, I cannot go beyond the commandment of the Lord, to do either good or bad of mine own mind; but what the Lord saith, that will I speak?"* (Numbers 23:27-30; Numbers 24:1-13)

Balaam's Prophecy of the Messiah

"And now, behold, I go unto my people: come therefore, and I will advertise thee what this people shall do to thy people in the latter days. And he took up a parable, and said, Balaam the son of Beor hath said, and the man whose eyes are open...He hath said, which heard the words of God, and knew the knowledge of the most High, which saw the vision of the Almighty, falling into a trance, but having his eyes open: I shall see him, but not now: <u>I shall behold him, but not nigh: there shall come a Star out of Jacob, and a Sceptre shall rise out of Israel</u> and shall smite the corners of Moab, and destroy all the children of Sheth. And Edom shall be a possession, Seir also shall be a possession for his enemies; and Israel shall do valiantly. Out of Jacob shall come he that shall destroy him that remaineth of the city."
(Numbers 25:14-19)

God's Anger with Balaam

Up to this point, we have seen the mountains, the earth, water, and animals bow at the presence of God. Now, Balaam's donkey saw the Lord and backed away. Balaam and his donkey got a kick-in-the pants for disobeying God. One morning, Balaam took it upon himself, to accompany Balak's princes to Moab; but God told Balaam the night before, *"If the men come to call thee, rise up, and go with them; but yet the word which I shall say unto thee, that shalt thou do."*
(Numbers 22:20)

Caption: **Balaam, his talking ass (Miss Chamora), and the Angel of the Lord.**

However, man can be so hasty because he wants to be in charge of himself. Because of his fame and reputation as a "seer," Balaam was out-of-control. Never the less, Balaam got much more than he asked for, ***"And God's anger was kindled because he [Balaam] went: and the angel of the Lord stood in the way for an adversary against him. Now he was riding upon his ass, and his two servants were with him. And the ass saw the angel of the Lord standing in the way, and his sword drawn in his hand: and the ass turned aside out of the way, and went into the field: and Balaam smite the ass, to turn her into the way. But the angel of the Lord stood in a path of the vineyards, a wall being on this side, and a wall on that side. And when the ass saw the angel of the Lord, she thrust herself unto the wall, and crushed Balaam's foot against the wall: and he smote her again. And the angel of the Lord went further, and stood in a narrow place, where was no way to turn either to the right hand or to the left. And when the ass saw the angel of the Lord, she fell down under Balaam: and Balaam's anger was kindled, and he smote the ass with a staff. And the angel of the Lord opened the mouth of the ass, and she said unto Balaam, What have I done unto thee, that thou has smitten me these three times? And Balaam said unto the ass, Because thou has mocked me: I would there were a sword in mine hand, for now would I kill thee. And the ass said unto Balaam, Am not I thing ass, upon which thou has ridden ever since I was thine unto this day? Was I ever wont to do so unto thee? And he said, Nay.*** [BY THIS TIME BALAAM SHOULD HAVE REALIZED THAT HE WAS TALKING TO AN ASS] ***Then the Lord opened the eyes of Balaam, and he saw the angel of the Lord standing in the way, and his sword drawn in his hand: and he bowed down his head, and fell flat on his face. And the angel of the Lord said unto him, Wherefore has thou smitten thine ass these three times? Behold, I went out to withstand thee, because thy way is perverse before me: And the ass saw me, and turned from me these three time: unless she had turned from me, surely now also I had slain thee, and saved her alive. And Balaam said unto the angel of the Lord, I have sinned; for I knew not that thou stoodest in the way against me: now therefore, if it displeases thee, I will get me back again. And the angel of the Lord said unto Balaam, Go with the men: but only the word that I shall speak unto thee, that thou shalt speak. So Balaam went with the princes of Balak."***
(Numbers 22:22-35)

Seen and Unseen

There is a spirit world, mostly unseen by human eyes, but it can manifest itself as God wills it. The Bible teaches us that there are three spiritual and physical worlds: heaven, earth, and hell (the underworld). As Christians, we know that God rules over all of His creation seen and unseen.

The Devil Exists

In the Book of Job 1:6, it states, *"Now there was a day when the sons of God came to present themselves before the Lord, and Satan came also among them. And the Lord said unto Satan, Whence comest thou? Then Satan answered the Lord, and said, From going to and fro in the earth, and from walking up and down in it."*

Jesus is Lord

In the New Testament, Apostle Paul tells us, *"That at the name of Jesus every knee should bow, of things in heaven, and things in earth, and things under the earth.. And that every tongue should confess that Jesus Christ is Lord, to the glory of God the Father."* (Philippians 2:10-11) Assuredly, Apostle Paul tells us that *"...we have redemption through his [Christ's] blood, even the forgiveness of sins."* (Colossians 1:14) Again, Apostle Paul states, *"For by him were all things created that are in heaven and that are in earth, visible and invisible, whether they be thrones, or dominions, or principalities, or powers: all things were created by him, and for him. And he is before all things and by him all things consist. And he is the head of the body, the church: who is the beginning, the firstborn from the dead: that in all things he might have the pre-eminence. For it pleased the Father that in him should all fullness dwell. And having made peace through the blood of his cross, by him to reconcile all things unto himself; by him, I say whether they be things in earth, or things in heaven. And you that were sometime alienated and enemies in your mind by wicked works, yet now hath he reconciled. In the body of his flesh through death, to present you holy and unblameable and unreproveable in his sight."* (Colossians1:16-22)

Chapter Six

Ancient Jericho

"...Go view the land, <u>especially Jericho</u>..." (Joshua 2:1)

In the Old Testament, ancient Jericho is one of the oldest cities in the world and (perhaps) the most prominent city in the valley of Jordan because of its location as the gateway to Western Palestine. Jericho is located about ten miles or more from the Dead Sea, four to five miles west from the Jordan River, and about fifteen to seventeen miles northeast of Jerusalem. The *first* mention of the city of Jericho appeared in the Old Testament.

According to multiple archaeologists and the results of many excavations, Jericho's history dates back to 9000 BC the later part of a Stone Age, continuing into the New Stone Age (Neolithic cultures about 7000 BC), through the Bronze Age, Iron Age, and Cooper Age (Chalcolithic) to this present day. People have consistently inhabited Jericho and archaeologists have documented this as fact. Through out all of these periods, there is one common denominator – the usage of mudbricks and stone in buildings and walls. To varying degrees (whether primitive, sophisticated, or complex), each settlement used vase amounts of stones to make tools (such as stone axes) large towers, buildings made of mudbricks and stone, stone foundations, floors made of terrazzo (burnt lime stone and clay colored in a red or pinkish tint and later the entire floor was polished), and mudbricks and stoned walls surrounding the settlement for protection to keep out intruders and warriors.

On record, archaeologists have dated the *fall of Jericho* (to be discussed later) about 1400 BC confirming the biblical story of Joshua and the children of Israel. A massive and well-fortified wall of stones surrounded Jericho.

Caption: Jericho.

Caption: Ancient Wall.

Meanings of Jericho

By definition, Jericho has a few very interesting meanings. Firstly, Jericho is known as the *"moon city."* The city itself is shaped like the crescent moon in its first quarter or like an amphitheater or elliptical-oblong with rounded ends. The residents of Jericho worshipped the *moon god and the host of heaven.*

Secondly, Jericho is known as the *"city of fragrance"* and the *"city of palm trees."* (Deuteronomy 34:3; Judges 1:16; 3:13) The perfumed fragrance comes from the "sap" and the fruit of the palm trees as well as the sap from the other trees and flowers. The air is filled with an exotic/sweet fragrance. The palm tree's sap was used to make strong drink (in modern terms, an alcoholic beverage). The process of collecting the "sap" from the palm tree is called "tapping." Cut the flower of the palm tree and attach a container or large jug to the flower for the liquid sap to drain into. Once the "tapping" process is complete, the sap can be: (1) refrigerated and dosed with a little "lime" to prevent fermentation; and (2) allowed to sit for a few hours - fermentation sets in and produces the fragrant aroma of wine. The longer the sap sits, the longer it ferments which produces either an intoxicating beverage, wine (sweet or sour), or vinegar. Certainly, the sap was used in many different ways (including cooking) and the entire palm tree itself (the fruit, seeds, and leaves) was put to productive use. For instance, the seeds were fed to camels, the fruit was eaten, the leaves were used to weave baskets and make fences, and the wood was used to build things and for fire wood.

The palm tree can grow to various heights from 15 feet to 89 feet or more. A huge grove of palm trees, other fruit trees, and exotic flowers surround Jericho.

Looking down from the top of a mountain, the city of Jericho was an oasis of palm trees and a beautiful site to behold. When Moses was about to die, God showed him the "Promised Land" and *the city of palm trees.* **"And Moses went up from the plains of Moab unto the mountain of Nebo, to the top of Pisgah, that is over against Jericho. And the Lord shewed him all the land of Gilead, unto Dan. And all Naphtali, and the land of Ephraim, and Manasseh, and all the land of Judah, unto the utmost sea. And the south, and the plan of the valley of Jericho, <u>the city of palm trees</u>, unto Zoar. And the Lord said unto him, This is the**

Caption: Oasis with palm trees.

land which I sware unto Abraham, unto Isaac, and unto Jacob, saying I will give it unto they seed: I have caused thee to see it with thine eyes, but thou shalt not go over thither. So Moses the servant of the Lord died there in the land of Moab, according to the word of the Lord. And he [the Lord] buried him in a valley in the land of Moab over against Beth-peor: but no man knoweth of his sepulcher unto this day. And Moses was an hundred and twenty years old when he died: his eye was not dim, nor his natural force abated."
(Deuteronomy 34:1-7)

Biblically, the palm tree represents ***"the righteous children of God" and "victory."*** Generally, the palm tree grows straight upward towards heaven. When the palm tree is loaded (or burdened) with fruit, it bends downward toward the earth as if it is bowing before His Majesty. The point is the palm tree does not break in half pieces because of the load or the natural forces that come against it. First Peter 5:6-7 states, ***"Humble yourselves therefore under the mighty hand of God that he may exalt you in due time. Casting all your care upon him for he careth for you."*** In Revelation 7:9, Apostle John saw ***"…all nations, kindreds, people, and tongues clothed with white robes and <u>palms in their hands</u>** [the sign of victory] **and standing before the throne and the Lamb…crying with a loud voice saying, Salvation to our God which sitteth upon the throne, and unto the Lamb."*** As a word of comment, some people do not think it is appropriate to *"cry out aloud"* or *"be emotional (singing, hand-clapping, dancing, and shouting) in church."* But, in the Book of Revelation, the saints are doing all of the above with *"no shame"* plus waiving the leaves of the palm trees! Well, if the saints can *"Praise the Lord"* before the Throne of God, then, they can *"Praise the Lord"* here on earth that belongs to God!

According to Psalm 92:12-14, ***"<u>The righteous shall flourish like the palm tree</u>: he shall grow like a cedar in Lebanon. Those that be planted in the house of the Lord shall flourish in the courts of our God. They shall still bring forth fruit in old age; they shall be fat and flourishing."*** It can be said that those who trust in the Lord will flourish – God will give them increase (fruit) and they will not lack anything. Also, the righteous will have long life like the beautiful cedar trees of Lebanon.

Proverbs 12:12-14 states, **"*...the root of the righteous yieldeth fruit...a man shall be satisfied with good by the fruit of his mouth...*"** Praise the Lord! The fruit of the palm tree is nutritious and the *"spiritual fruit"* of the righteous should be just as nutritious, i.e., ten-fold, fifty-fold, or one-hundred-fold. It is said that the "female" palm trees produce tons of fruit each year. Therefore, *the righteous people of God* should share the "gospel" *(the good news)* that Jesus (the Savior) is alive, risen from the dead, and sitting on the right side of the Throne of God, and *"the plan of salvation"* is for everyone. Colossians 1:10 states **"*...walk worthy of the Lord unto all pleasing, <u>being fruitful in every good work, and increasing in the knowledge of God.</u>*"**

In spite of the *lack of water in the wilderness*, the palm trees' roots are buried deep within the earth and they are watered by an underground spring. [27] Like the palm tree, the righteous children of God are *"hidden and buried"* in the Christ, and He is their shield and buckler in the times of trouble. John 7:37-38 states, **"*If any man thirst, let him come unto me, and drink. He that believeth on me, as the scripture hath said, out of his belly shall flow rivers of living water.*"** Believers drink spiritual water and it is a marvelous energizer! God Himself patents this spiritual drink! The only way to get this *spiritual beverage* is through Jesus Christ and there is no other way!

Carved Palm Trees - Solomon's Temple

According to the Bible, king Solomon (means *"peaceable"*) decorated the Temple with carved palm trees and carved open flowers. After the death of his father (king David), king Solomon requested his friend Hiram (king of Tyre) to send the best timber of cedar (trees of Lebanon) and timber of fir to build the House of the Lord. So, king Hiram sent all that Solomon requested by sea in floats. (I Kings 5:6-10) King Solomon made a league with king Hiram; so they were at peace. Moreover, Solomon paid Hiram handsomely for the timbers and laborers. All of the timbers

---

[27]   According to II Kings 2:18-22, Elisha healed the waters of Jericho. He went to the spring of the water and poured in salt from a new cruse (flat metal dish) and said, *"**Thus saith the Lord, I have healed these waters; there shall not be from thence any more death or barren land. So the waters were healed unto this day, according to the saying of Elisha.**"*

and stones were cut to the exact measurement, brought in, and put in place, *"...so that there was neither hammer no ax nor any tool of iron heard in the house, while it was in building."* (I Kings 6:7)

The temple was magnificent and decorated with all sorts of carvings that were overlaid with gold! In reference to the timbers, I Kings 6:15, 29-35 states, *"And he [Solomon] built the walls of the house within with boards of cedar, both the floor of the house, and the walls of the ceiling: And he covered them on the inside with wood, and covered the floor of the house with planks of fir...<u>And he carved all the walls of the house round about with carved figures of cherubims and palm trees and open flowers</u>, within and without. And the floor of the house he overlaid with gold, within and without...And for the entering of the oracle he made doors of olive tree: the lintel and side posts were a fifth part of the wall. The two doors also were of olive tree; <u>and he carved upon them carvings of cherubims and palm trees and open flowers, and overlaid them with gold, and spread gold upon the cherubims, and upon the palm trees</u>. So also made he for the door of the temple posts of olive tree, a fourth part of the wall. And the two doors were of fir tree: the two leaves of the one door were folding, and the two leaves of the other door were folding. <u>And he carved thereon cherubims and palm trees and open flowers</u>: and covered them with gold fitted upon the carved work."*

Accursed Jericho of Canaan

Jericho was part of the region or "land of Canaan" and full of iniquity. Since Rahab was from Jericho, let us pick on Jericho. In Joshua's own words the city of Jericho was **DAMNED**, *"<u>And the city shall be accused, even it, and all that are therein, to the Lord...Keep yourselves from the accursed thing, lest ye make yourselves accursed and make the camp of Israel a curse, and trouble it...</u>"* (Joshua 6:17-18)

The entire "land of Canaan" was plagued with **SIN, SIN, SIN, and SIN:**

(1)   Homosexuality (Genesis 13:13; 19:1-38; Leviticus 18:22-30; 20:13);

(2)   Incest (Leviticus 18:6-40; 20:10-23);

(3)   Inordinate affection (Leviticus 18:19-30; 20:18-23);

(4)   Adultery (Leviticus 18:20-30; 20:10-23);

(5)   Idolatry (Leviticus 18:21:30; 20:2-5; Deuteronomy 12);

(6)   Profanity (Leviticus 18:21-30);

(7)   Beastiality (Leviticus 18:23-30; 20:15-23);

(8)   Witchcraft (Leviticus 20:6, 23; Deuteronomy 18:9-14);

(9)   Whoredom (Leviticus 20:1-23);

(10)   Dishonor to parents (Leviticus 20:9-23);

(11)   Murder (Deuteronomy 12:31; 18:9-14);

(12)   Stealing (Leviticus 19:11-13; 20:23); and

(13)   Lying (Leviticus 19:11-16; 20:23)

Caption: Ancient temple entrance.

False Worship

The moon god and host of heaven

Like the Egyptians, the residents of Jericho (the *"moon city")* worshiped the *"moon god"* and *"the host of heaven"* [28] (the sun, moon and stars).

Of course, Abraham spoke of the judge and idolatry worshippers, ***"Shall not the Judge of all the earth do right? And the Lord said, If I find in Sodom fifty*** [29] ***righteous within the city, then I will spare all the place for their sakes..."*** (Genesis 18:25-26) Like his *grandfather* (Abraham), Job hated idolatry. Job was the sixth son of Issachar (Abraham's son). Job (means *"afflicted")* declared his innocence of sin and idolatry worship to the sun and the moon, ***"If I beheld the sun when it shines, or the moon waking in brightness: And my heart hath been secretly enticed, or my mouth hath kissed my hand: This also were an iniquity to be punished by the judge: for I should have denied the God that is above."*** (Job 31:26-28)

In II Kings 23:5-6, Josiah (the king of Judah) did away with the high places of idolatry worship, ***"He put down the idolatrous priests whom the kings of Judah had ordained to burn incense in the high places in the cities of Judah, and in places round about Jerusalem; them also that burned incense unto Baal, to the sun, and to the moon, and to the planets, and to all the host of heaven. And he brought out the grove from the house of the Lord, without Jerusalem unto the brook Kidron, and burned it at the brook Kidron, and stamped it small to powder, and cast the powder thereon upon the graves of the children of the people."***

In Psalm 104:19, God's greatness is declared over many things including the sun and moon, ***"He appointed the moon for seasons: the sun knoweth his going down..."*** [30] God did not tell man to worship the host of heaven. In Joshua 10:12-13,

---

[28]   The army of the skies: the sun (king); the moon (vice-regent to the sun); the stars and planets (the attendants).

[29]   Eventually the total number of righteous to be spared from destruction dropped from fifty to ten. Unfortunately, Abraham did not go lower than ten.

[30]   The Solaric Covenant (Genesis 1:14-19; 8:22; Jeremiah 33:20; Daniel 2:21).

God proved His Omnipotence over the sun and the moon through another miracle, ***"Then spake Joshua to the Lord in the day when the Lord delivered up the Amorites before the children of Israel, and he said in the sight of Israel, Sun, stand thou still upon Gibeon; and thou, Moon, in the valley of Ajalon.*** [31] ***<u>And the sun stood still, and the moon stayed until the people had avenged themselves upon their enemies. Is not written in the book of Jasher? So the sun stood still in the midst of heaven, and hasted not to go down about a whole day. And there was no day like that before it or after it, that the Lord hearkened unto the voice of a man: for the Lord fought for Israel."</u>***

<u>*Baal and Asherah*</u>

Like the other nations of Canaan, the residents of Jericho worshipped Baal, Asherah, and other false gods. In fact, all of the inhabitants in the Promised Land worshipped false gods.

By definition, Baal (a masculine god) means *"lord or master."* He was the Canaanite sun god of fertility, nature, growth, rain, and reproduction. In addition to Baal, the Canaanites worshiped Asherah (a feminine goddess) the "mother goddess" or the "queen of heaven." Worship of Canaanite gods included sexual immorality, wild behavior, ceremonial acts, and many other things. There was no limit to the perpetrator's lewdness, impropriety, or impurity with children and others (regardless of the sexuality).

Like the heathens, the nonconforming and backslidden children of Israel worshipped the *"queen of heaven"* and they practiced sexual misconduct, lewd behavior, and abominable immorality. God was not pleased with the sin of His chosen people. In Jeremiah 7:17, it states, ***<u>"Seest thou not what they do in the cities of Judah and in the streets of Jerusalem. The children gather wood, and the fathers kindle the fire, and the women knead their dough, to make cakes to the queen of heaven, and to pour out drink offering unto other gods, that they may provoke me to anger."</u>*** Furthermore, Jeremiah 44:17 states, that false

---

[31] Ajalon was a city in the valley of Ajalon (between Jerusalem and Ekron). II Chronicles 38:18. While the sun was setting and the moon was rising, Joshua ordered them both to stand still until the battle was won.

worship was not only limited to the people - it included the leaders, *"But, <u>we will</u> <u>certainly do whatsoever thing that goeth forth out of our own mouth, to burn</u> <u>incense unto the queen of heaven, and to pour out drink offerings unto her, as</u> <u>we have done, we and our fathers, our kings, and our princes, in the cities of</u> <u>Judah, and in the streets of Jerusalem: for then had we plenty of victuals and</u> <u>were well, and saw no evil</u>."*

Apostle Luke puts in his say about the children of Israel's rebellion (against God and Moses) during their forty year wandering in the wilderness. *"This is he [Moses] that was in the church in the wilderness with the angel which spake to him in the mount Sinai...who received the lively oracles...to whom our fathers would not obey...In their hearts turned back again into Egypt, saying unto Aaron, Make us gods to go before us: for as for this Moses, which brought us out of the land of Egypt, we wot not what is become of him. And they made a calf in those days, and offered sacrifice unto the idol, and rejoiced in the works of their own hands. <u>Then God turned, and gave them up to worship the host of heaven</u>; as it is written in the book of prophets, O ye house of Israel, have ye offered to me slain beasts and sacrifices by the space of forty years in the wilderness? Yea, ye took up the tabernacle of Moloch [Ammonite god], and the star of your god Remphan [sun god], figures which ye made to worship them: and I will carry you away beyond Babylon...Our fathers had the tabernacle of witness in the wilderness, as he appointed, speaking unto Moses..."* (Acts 7:38-44)

Children in Ancient Jericho

In ancient Jericho (as in the land of Canaan) children did not have normal happy lives, as children should. They lived in *dens of iniquity* and they had to learn how to cope with horrible circumstances. There was no child protection services or foster care homes for them to hide under. If such an organization existed, the people in charge of these services were just as corrupt as the parents of the children. Truthfully, the children were dishonest because *they learned sinful* behavior and corruption from their parents and others. There was no righteousness. So, children grew up quickly and deceitfully. At an early age, they had to survive in a pagan society in an accursed city. Perhaps, children (born into rich and moderately middle class families) had privileges that less fortunate children lacked. However, this does not mean the rich and middle classes were excluded from corruption. Instead, the wealthy and modest families had more means to buy more corruption and pleasures. Similarly, poorer parents were just as corrupt, but they did not have the funds to squander on "dirty toys" as the rich did. Certainly having children must have brought a certain amount of joy to the rich and poor. After the newness of the birth wore off, the need to put food on the table became paramount and a reality in poorer classes. In all cases (rich to poor families), the children continued the bloodline of their parents.

Generally, the father or patriarch of a family passed on his blessing [32] to the eldest son who passed on the blessing to his son and so forth. Rich parents passed on the family's fortunes and assets (including their pagan beliefs) to the next generation. Likewise, middle class parents passed on their current occupation (and religious beliefs) as candlestick makers, bakers, fishermen, dressmakers, or whatever the trade to their son. In poorer families, the father passed on his poverty and pagan beliefs to his son.

Only the males were educated by their parents or allowed to attend school. Wealthy parents sent their sons to school and middle class parents educated their sons at home while adjusting work and training schedules. Parents cannot teach children what they do not know. They can only educate their children to the extent of their knowledge, experience, and understanding. Boys were the primary targets for training and education because they had to continue the family's name, trade, and/or business. Based on tradition, girls were not allowed to attend school. There was no school for rich or poor girls. In some cases, rich girls had nannies or female attendants. Quite possibly, some parents provided their daughters (in the absence of sons) with primitive education and training concerning the family's business or trade.

Child Labor

In general, there were no righteous laws in the city of Jericho. Thus, there were <u>no laws governing child labor</u>. In Eastern culture, children (like women) were considered chattel. Children from middle to lower class families were forced to work all sorts

---

[32]   Abraham, Isaac, and Jacob

of jobs small and large. Families were large (no birth control) and there was not enough money to house and feed everyone. The extended family (that included grandparents, aunts, uncles, sick relatives, related orphans, and others) meant extra mouths to feed. So, the children were put to work to bring in financial support to their parents. Every working body was expected to bring home money, food, stolen goods, or *something else* to supplement the family's income. In fact, children had no more rights than dogs. If a needy family had twelve children, then, all twelve children could be put to work.

Child Prostitution

In many cases, children were sold into religious prostitution as sexual slaves (at a very early age) to the priest or priestess of *pagan temples* or *sold into bondage,* or to other *houses of sin.* For example, children could be sold or donated to the house of Baal (a pagan god) by the parents hoping for financial gain, favor with the priest or priestess, or some other gratuity.

At a very early age, children were not only robbed of their innocence and rights, and they were taught unnatural behavior which they (in turn) perpetuated with others. Frankly, they were demonized and they carried home-learned filthy behavior to reenact on smaller children, whomever, or whatever. This behavior created the vilest of children and the vilest of home life because the parents participated in the same rituals. Therefore, the entire family was corrupt.

Child Sacrifice

Children were sacrificed as gifts and burned at the altars of pagan gods. In doing so, parents were giving up the most prized possession (their children) and their future. The Canaanites offered up their children, baked cakes, and burned incense to Baal, Asherah, the moon god, the host of heaven, and other false deities. Firstly, they believed that this was the right way to please the gods who *(they erroneously believed)* gave them their children along with everything else. Secondly, this confirmed the fact that Canaanite children had no democratic rights and *that their lives had no usefulness* other than to be sexual slaves or burned at the stakes. Moreover, the Canaanites provoked the Almighty God to wrath!

During the reign of king Josiah of Judah (as stated earlier), he took the groves (the gods of Baal, Asherah, and other gods whose figures were carved on the "tree trunks) out of the house of the Lord and he burned them, ground the ashes to "fine" powder, and threw the ashes on the graves of their children who had been offered as sacrifices to the false gods. (II Kings 23:6-7)

Chapter Seven

The Almighty God

"Hear, O Israel: the Lord our God is one Lord: And thou shalt love the Lord thy God with all thine heart, and with all thy soul, and with all thy might. And these words, which I command thee this day, shall be in thine heart: And thou shalt teach them diligently unto thy children, and shalt talk of them when thou sittest in thine house, and when thou walkest by the way, and when thou liest down, and when thou risest up. And thou shalt bind them for a sign upon thine hand, and they shall be as frontlets between thine eyes. And thou shalt write them upon the posts of thy house, and on thy gates." (Deut. 6:4-9)

The patriarchs (Abraham, Isaac, and Jacob) knew God as *El Shaddai (the Almighty God)*, *"...the Lord appeared to Abram, and said unto him, I am the Almighty God; walk before me and be thou perfect..."* (Gen. 17:1) In this light, God is the strong one, fruitful one, bountiful one, and nourishing one. In Exodus 6:3, God said, *"I appeared unto Abraham, unto Isaac, and unto Jacob, by the name of God Almighty, but by my name Jehovah was I not known to them."* [33]

In Exodus 3:14, God revealed Himself to Moses as, *"...I AM WHO I AM..."* In Hebrew this is *"Ehyeh asher Ehyeh"* meaning *"I am the One who Was, and Is, and Is to come."*

Jehovah (means *"the Eternal Creator"* or *"self-existent"*) is *Yahweh* (YHWH) *"My Lord" or "The Lord "* - *Yahweh* is exclusive to Israel. A proper pronunciation

---

[33]   In Christianity, we know Him as Jehovah God, the covenant God of the Hebrews.

for Yahweh is Yehowah. The Hebrews only pronounced His name once a year on the *day of atonement*. According to Leviticus 24:16, ***"He that blasphemeth the name of the Lord shall surely be put to death..."*** For whatever reason, the Hebrews were afraid to utter His name. Do not be alarmed! The Hebrews wrote YHWH but pronounced *Adonai* (meaning *"My Lord Jehovah"*). Another spelling for *Adonai* is *Adonay.* Other titles are: Jehovah-Elohim; Adonai-Jehovah; Jehovah-Jireh; Jehovah-Shalom; Jehovah-Ropheka; Jehovah-Nissi; Jehovah-Tsidkeenu; Jehovah-Mekaddishkem; Jehovah-Saboath; Jehovah-Shammah; Jehovah-Elyon; Jehovah-Rohi; Jehovah-Hoseenu; Jehovah-Eloheka; and Jehovah-Elohay.

Psalm 104 – God's Greatness

"Bless the Lord, O my soul. O Lord my God, thou art very great; thou art clothed with honor and majesty. Who coverest thyself with light as with a garment: who stretchest out the heavens like a curtain. Who layeth the beams of his chambers in the waters: who maketh the clouds his chariot: who walketh upon the wings of the wind: Who maketh his angels spirits; his ministers a flaming fire: Who laid the foundations of the earth, that it should not be removed for ever.

Thou coverest it with the deep as with a garment: the waters stood above the mountains. At thy rebuke they fled; at the voice of thy thunder they hasted away. They go up by the mountains; they go down by the valleys unto the place which thou hast founded for them. Thou hast set a bound that they may not pass over; that they turn not again to cover the earth. He sendeth the springs into the valleys, which run among the hills. They give drink to every beast of the field: the wild asses quench their thirst. By them shall the fowls of the heaven have their habitation, which sing among the branches. He watereth the hills from his chambers: the earth is satisfied with the fruit of thy works.

He causeth the grass to grow for the cattle, and herb for the service of man: that he may bring forth food out of the earth; And wine that maketh glad the heart of man, and oil to make his face to shine, and bread which strengtheneth man's heart. The trees of the Lord are full of sap; the cedars of Lebanon, which he hath planted; Where the birds make their nests: as for the stork, the fir trees are her house. The high hills are a refuge for the wild goats; and the rocks for the conies.

He appointed the moon for seasons: the sun knoweth his going down. Thou makest darkness, and it is night: wherein all the beasts of the forest do creep forth. The young lions roar after their prey, and seek their meat from God. The sun ariseth, they gather themselves together and lay them down in their dens. Man goeth forth unto his work and to his labor until the evening.

O Lord, How manifold are thy works! In wisdom has thou made them all: the earth is full of thy riches. So is this great and wide sea, wherein are things creeping innumerable, both small and great beasts. There go the ships: there is that leviathan, whom thou has made to play therein. These wait all upon thee; that thou mayest give them their meat in due season. That thou givest them they gather: thou openest thine hand, they are filled with good. Thou hidest thy face, they are troubled: thou takest away their breath, they die, and return to their dust. Thou sendest forth thy spirit, they are created: and thou renewest the face of the earth. The glory of the Lord shall endure forever: the Lord shall rejoice in his works. He looketh on the earth, and it trembleth: he toucheth the hills, and they smoke.

I will sing unto the Lord as long as I live: I will sing praise to my God while I have my being. My meditation of him shall be sweet: I will be glad in the Lord. Let the sinners be consumed out of the earth, and let the wicked be no more. Bless thou the Lord, O my soul. PRAISE YE THE LORD!"

God's Charge to Israel

"Hear therefore, O Israel, and observe to do it; that it may be well with thee, and that ye may increase mightily, as the Lord God of thy fathers hath promised thee, in the land that floweth with milk and honey." (Deuteronomy 6:3)

"And it shall be, when The Lord thy God shall have brought thee into the land which he sware unto thy fathers, to Abraham, to Isaac, and to Jacob, to give thee great and goodly cities, which thou buildest not, And houses full of all good things, which thou filledst not, and wells digged which thou diggedst not, vineyards and olive trees, which thou plantedst not; when thou shalt have eaten and be full..." (Deuteronomy 6:10-11)

"For the land whether thou goest in to possess it, is not as the land of Egypt, from whence ye came out, where thou sowedst thy seed, and wateredst it with thy foot, as a garden of herbs: But the land whither ye go to possess it, is a land of hills and valleys, and drinketh water of the rain of heaven: A land which the Lord thy God careth for: the eyes of the Lord thy God are always upon it, from the beginning of the year even unto the end of the year."
(Deuteronomy 11:10-12)

"And it shall come to pass, if ye shall hearken diligently unto my [Moses] commandments which I command you this day, to love the Lord your God, and to serve him with all you heart and with all your soul. That I will give you the rain of your land in his due season, the first rain, and the latter rain, that thou mayest gather in thy corn, and thy wine, and thine oil. And I will send grass in thy fields for thy cattle, that thou mayest eat and be full."
(Deuteronomy 11:13-15)

"Take heed to yourselves, that your heart be not deceived, and ye turn aside, and serve other gods, and worship them: And then the Lord's wrath be kindled against you, and he shut up the heaven, that there be no rain, and that the land yield not her fruit; and lest ye perish quickly from off the good land which the Lord giveth you." (Deuteronomy 11:16-17)

God - Keeper of His Word

"The Lord did not set his love upon you [Israel], nor choose you, because ye were more in number than any people; for ye were the fewest of all people: But because the Lord loved you, and because he would keep the oath which he had

sworn unto your fathers [Abraham, Isaac, and Jacob], hath the Lord brought you out with a mighty hand, and redeemed you out of the house of bondmen, from the hand of Pharaoh king of Egypt. Know therefore that the Lord thy God, he is God, the faithful God, which keepeth covenant and mercy with them that love him and keep his commandments to a thousand generations; And repayeth them that hate him to their face, to destroy them: he will not be slack to him that hateth him, he will repay him to his face."

(Deuteronomy 7:7-10)

Chapter Eight

Rahab's Childhood

One of the little girls in the city of Jericho was called, **Rahab**. Let us assume (based upon the social structures and the immoral practices in Jericho) that Rahab was an unhappy child. She lived with her parents, brothers, and sisters in poverty (one of the poorest ghetto districts) of Jericho. Her father was ill mannered, and most of the time, unemployed. Her mother (under the influence of an ignorant husband) was burdened with child bearing, taking care of kids, washing, cooking, and baking bread for vendors. Her mother was short, fat, and pudgy while the father was of medium height and build. They were preoccupied with many problems, especially, how to feed and clothe a large family.

The parents rented a small two-room apartment on the first floor of a three-story building. This little girl played outside by the door in the dirty streets of Jericho, but she always rubbed-off the dirt on her face – something inside told her to look pretty. Her toys were pebbles, stones, sticks, trash, and any whatnot that was thrown down into the streets. The streets were crowded with homeless beggars, orphan children, peddlers, thieves, unruly kids, stray animals, sick people lying in the streets and people buying and selling in the marketplace. Her playmates were stray cats and dogs. She watched many travelers pass by and wondered where they were going. Some of these travelers were dressed quite well and she was in awe of their garments. She had never seen clothing like that in deep reds of scarlet and purple robes. It was as if the pagan "gods" came down to earth. This was the only excitement and panorama in her life.

At nights, Rahab laid awake because she was hungry and cold. Most of the time, she cried herself to sleep without knowing why she was crying. She shared a bed with her brothers and sisters. But the bedding was pitiful – a poorly put together wood frame (with peg wooden legs), a mattress made from old rags and stuffed with straw bits, and pieces of old garments which made it quite uneven and lumpy. Being the eldest, she slept on the end with three rewards: (1) she was not squashed in the middle of the bed; (2) if one of her siblings lost his water during the night, she would not get soaked; and (3) she could get out of bed without crossing over her brothers and sisters. During the nights, she heard screams of torture, rape, and pleas for help from the streets. Inside the building, she heard echoes of moaning and groaning throughout the building *and this was her childhood lullaby.*

Generally, mothers and grandmothers hold babies and small children in their arms close to their breasts and these little ones were lulled to sleep with harmonic tunes. But this little girl listened to the many horrors throughout the night and her dreams were filled with fear, frustrations, and nightmares.

The Young Rahab

According to Jewish history, **<u>Rahab was ten years old</u>** at the time of Israel's mass exodus from Egypt. Quite possibly, Rahab worked to supply extra income for her parents. Rahab was quite mature for a ten year old. If so, she got up each morning at 7:30AM for an eight-hour day of labor. Let us assume she worked at *Jericho Inn* to perform many duties such as cleaning the kitchen, wiping tables and chairs, sweeping and scrubbing floors, making beds, drawing buckets of water from the well, plucking chicken feathers, gathering hen eggs, and feeding the livestock. Life was not easy for a small girl who worked at a particular inn filled with *"prostitutes and johns."*

By now, Rahab learned how to neatly braid her own hair, wash her face, hands, hair and skin, lie, steal, cheat, and to use profanity among other things. Keeping herself clean, outwardly, was a peculiar habit of hers. She learned about outer beauty from the travelers who passed by her home in the *ghetto* when she was just five years old. Back then, they use to pat her on the head and tell her that she was "pretty" But no one told her that inner beauty was more important than outward beauty. She over came the name-calling and unhappy words from the other kids as she rushed through the streets to *Jericho Inn.*

Caption: Ancient well with pillars and brick wall.

Caption: Ancient ruins.

Caption: Ancient interior with sunlight through ceiling.

The inn's prostitutes were the only *role models* for Rahab. They were part of the working class who made money, and more importantly, they just happen to be women. In her own way, Rahab was a working girl that looked forward to her wages and tips. On good days, the prostitutes gave handsome tips to Rahab and this was a bonus and a great incentive. This added income made Rahab's parents very happy and they did not care how Rahab earned extra money. From time to time, the prostitutes gave their discarded clothing to Rahab! Now, she owned three changes of clothing and two pairs of sandals. Naturally, their clothing was too large but one day Rahab would soon grow into them and much more! All the more, these gifts solidified Rahab's appreciation for the prostitutes because no one ever did anything for her and no one seemed to care about her.

During her lunchtime, Rahab listened to the prostitutes' cackle and stories about their customers. Some of the regular *johns* looked funny to Rahab because they wrapped their heads up to hide their faces and some left out of the kitchen and back doors.

On a few occasions, a few prostitutes got big bellies, and eventually, a baby came out! Immediately, Rahab knew that these prostitutes became mothers like her own mother who gave birth to Rahab's brothers and sisters. But then, the babies disappeared from the *inn* and were housed in a boarding house on a back street. One day, the innkeeper ordered young Rahab to deliver extra food to the boarding house where the babies were kept. Upon entering, she saw dozens of babies, infants, and children. She was shocked because it seemed unnatural to see more than six kids in one house. Some of the babies were sick and some were healthy, crawling around, and giggling as babies do. The toddlers, about two to three years old, were hitting one another and walking around. The five year olds starred at Rahab, a newcomer into their environment. Rahab spoke to some of them because they seemed to be drawn to her. Amazingly, Rahab had *compassion* on these kids because she remembered her childhood of 5 years old and under.

Chapter Nine

"And Joshua the son of Nun sent two men secretly from Shittim as spies, saying, "Go view the land, especially Jericho...." <u>*And they went and came into the house of a harlot whose name was Rahab, and lodged there*</u>. (Joshua 2:1)

Rahab – the Harlot

By definition, Rahab's name has several meanings: (1) broad; (2) arrogant; (3) sea monster, dragon of the sea, demon; and (4) symbolic of Egypt and Babylon. It was said that Rahab was beautiful and stunning as a full-grown woman. As states earlier, she was ten years old during Israel's wandering in the wilderness. By the time Joshua and the children of Israel crossed the Jordan River, Rahab was about fifty (50) years old and ageless.

Rahab was adorned in jewels (all sorts of precious stones and pearls) given to her as gifts by the king, top officials, and her wealthy customers. It was her style to wear five to seven multiple ropes of fresh-water pearls around her neck, gold and silver bangles on her wrist, and a huge three-quarter inch two-headed snake *gold* bangle (with eyes made of emeralds) on both of her upper arms. She had long flowing wavy black hair with light green "cat-like" eyes that peered into the lustful souls of men. Her favorite colors were red, purple, deep blue, and gold. She painted charcoal black eyeliner on her upper and lower eyelids. In Eastern culture, it was proper for women to make their eyes seem larger. Whenever Rahab left the *Inn*, she covered her face and wrapped her body in less transparent clothing. Her body was slender, proportioned, and well kept because she bathed in precious oils and fragrances made from the *exotic flowers* and *sap* from the palm trees in Jericho. At night, she put mudpacks (taken from the Dead Sea) on her face to tighten and cleanse her pores.

Twice monthly, she dipped her entire body into hot mud baths to soothe her aching muscles and to rejuvenate her body. With the help of her *highly* paid maid, she was rubbed in *assorted scents* (dependant upon her moods) such as lilac, honeysuckle, lilies (fleur-de-lis), and sweet-sensuous opium fragrances. Then, Rahab dressed in the most transparent and seductive silks *hand-made* and imported from the Orient, Phoenicia, Egypt, and Babylon. Like her clothing, her long silk scarves were scented with fragrances and ornaments. As she walked her *golden* anklets (trimmed with miniature delicate bells) *jingled as if to proclaim her presence.* The aroma of her fragrances and oils left a trail behind her for desiring and lusting men to follow and that they did. Whenever business was slow, this is the way Rahab lured new customers to the Inn. This too was the trick of her trade. However, there is one thing for sure, **RAHAB WAS A HARLOT!** She was a master of seduction!

Broad

In Scripture, Rahab may be the first recorded female inn-keeper. According to the Bible, *Rahab's Inn* sat on top of the city's wall in Jericho. So, from her window, Rahab could see the road outside of the city's gate as well as the travelers coming into the city, the opening of the gate in the morning, and the closing of the gate at dusk.

There is no end to speculation concerning how Rahab became the inn-keeper. Perhaps, this was the same inn she worked in and grew up in as a child. Possibly, Rahab purchased this inn from its original owner. Maybe she was the *mistress or protégé* of the previous inn's owner. Perhaps, she saved up her money and bought the inn from the retiring owner. *Regardless*, God had a plan for Rahab's life.[34] Remember, God can use anyone and anything (whenever and wherever) as He pleases – **God is Omnipotent, Omnipresent, and Omniscient!**

Rahab is one of the most complicated and notorious[35] women in the Bible. She was *"The Inn-keeper"* of innkeepers. She had broad business sense because she had to cater to a large assortment of clientele. Factually, she was the proprietor of one

---

[34]   God has a plan for my life and for your life!
[35]   She is the first Jezebel.

Caption: Rahab talking to a client.

Caption: Ancient architecture.

Caption: Ancient architecture.

Caption: Window of ancient building ruins.

of the oldest professions in the world. Rahab was a professional whore and she was in the business to make money, to survive. In her world, Rahab's behavior was acceptable. Sin was rampant in Jericho. In order to please the gods, the Canaanites gave themselves over to pleasures of the flesh and they accepted each other's imperfections without judging one another. As the sole proprietor, it was Rahab's job to please her clients.

Basically, Rahab had the "411" on everyone. She had inside information regarding people, secrets, births (illegal and legitimate), politics, business opportunities, gossip, exploits, arrests, and imprisonment to say the least. Rahab had the first who's who list on everything. If ever there was an ancient inter-net-work, Rahab had the first one! Modern man knows the inter-net-work as the www.com database with all sorts of *broad information* (educational, scientific, political, medical, inspirational, and historical as well as *things* which are not healthy to discuss) and it is FILLED with PORNOGRAPHY! We are reminded that ***"The Lord spake to Moses in the plains of Moab by Jordan near Jericho…When ye are passed over Jordan into the land of Canaan: Then ye shall drive out all the inhabitants of the land from before you, and <u>destroy all their pictures</u>** [PORNOGRAPHY], **and destroy all their molten images, and quite pluck down all their high places; And ye shall dispossess the inhabitants of the land and dwell therein…"*** (Numbers 33:50-53) *Rahab's Inn* was the place to be on any night of the week. On pagan holidays, feasts, and new moons, Rahab held luxurious exotic parties and orgies. Their colors were bright purples and reds!

Since there is no mention of dilemmas or issues with other residents in Jericho; we can assume that Rahab had no enemies and that she got along with everybody. She seemed to be highly favored among people (rich and poor), clientele, business men, soldiers, married men, single men, priests, politicians, and even the king of Jericho knew Rahab. It was the king of Jericho who sent his soldiers to inquire about the visitors at *Rahab's Inn*.

<u>Arrogant</u>

By definition, arrogant means *(1) unduly or excessively proud; overbearing; and (2) characterized by haughtiness; and unreasonable.* Psalm 12:2 states that the proud are arrogant, ***<u>"They speak vanity every one with his neighbor: with flattering lips and with a double heart do they speak. The Lord shall cut off all flattering lips and the tongue that speaketh proud things: Who have said, With our tongue will we prevail; our lips are our own: who is lord over us</u>*?"** Rahab was guilty of self-importance, but the Bible states**, *"Whoso privily slandereth his neighbor, him will I cut off: him that hath an high look and a proud heart will not I suffer…He that worketh deceit shall not dwell within my house: he that telleth lies shall not tarry in my sight. I will early destroy all the wicked of the land; that I may cut off all wicked doers from the city of the Lord."*** (Psalm 101:5, 7-8)

<u>Sea Monster, Dragon of the Sea, Demon, Egypt</u>

In the Bible, Rahab's name is associated with many evils. Her name is mention in the same breath as a sea monster, dragon of the sea, demon, and even symbolic of kingdoms such as Egypt.

(Sea Monster, Dragon of the Sea, Demon…)

The Bible states, in II Timothy 3:13, ***"But evil men and seducers shall wax worse and worse, deceiving, and being deceived…"*** As a temptress, Rahab is a sea monster, dragon of the sea, Leviathan, and demon (possessed with an evil spirit). All of these descriptions are associated with water, turbulence, thunderstorms, rainstorms, fury, rage, injuries, crisis, death, and destruction. At first, innocent boaters are drawn to calm waters on beautiful sunny days; then comes a gale warning and next the hurricane is upon them out of nowhere. Being visual beings, men are drawn to *beautiful women.* [36] On the outside, these women may be as follows: good looking, in top shape, fancy dresser, slim shape, lips painted red, *freshly* arched eyebrows, and a winking eye. *Behind the "wink" is a "blink" = "a snake in the grass."*

---

[36]   There is nothing wrong with looking good, but make sure the inside is Godly.

God made beautiful women. Look at Job's daughters. Well. God took Job's first set of children but He gave him another set of good-looking kids. The conclusion of Job's life was greater than his beginning; ***"The Lord turned the captivity of Job, when he prayed for his friends. Also, the Lord gave Job twice as much as he had before…For he had fourteen thousand sheep, six thousand camels, thousand yoke of oxen, a thousand she asses. He had also seven sons and three daughters."*** (Job 42:10) All of Job's daughters are listed in the Old Testament (Jemima, Kezia, and Kerenhappuch) ***as beautiful women***. However, Job's youngest daughter wore *heavy* makeup. Kerenhappuch (means *"horn of the eye-paint"*) that referred to the cosmetic case the eye make up was stored in. Ancient women painted their eyes to make them look larger.

The sea monster, dragon of the sea, and the Leviathan awakes from his deep sleep. He arises to the surface to destroy its victims. He is none other than Satan (the great dragon)! Regarding the Leviathan, Job said, ***"Who can discover the face of his garment? Or who can come to him with his double bridle? He maketh the deep to boil like a pot: he maketh the sea like a pot of ointment. He maketh a path to shine after him; one would think the deep to be hoary. Upon earth there is not his like, who is made without fear. He beholdeth all high things: he is a king over all the children of pride."*** (Job 41)

Like the serpent that beguiled *Eve in the Garden of Eden*, Rahab allured her victims *"with flattering lips and the tongue that speaketh proud things."* Psalm 104:25-26 acknowledges God's greatness, ***"O Lord, how manifold are thy works! In wisdom hat thou made them all: the earth is full of thy riches. So is this great and wide sea, wherein are things creeping innumerable, both small and great beasts. There go the ships: there is that leviathan, whom thou has made to play therein."*** Psalm 74:12-17 states that God is King not the great dragon, ***"For God is my King of old, working salvation in the midst of the earth. Thou didst divide the sea by thy strength: thou brakest the heads of the dragons in the waters. Thou brakest the heads of the leviathan in pieces, and gavest him to be meat to the people inhabiting the wilderness. Thou didst cleave the fountain and the flood: thou driedst up mighty rivers. The day is thine, the night also is thine: thou hast prepared the light and the sun. Thou has set all the borders of*** *the earth: thou has made summer and winter."* Isaiah 51:9-10 states, *"Awake, awake, put on strength, O arm of the Lord; awake, as in the ancient days, in the generations of old. <u>Art thou not it that hath cut Rahab and wounded the dragon? Art thou not it that hath dried up the sea, the waters of the great deep; that hath made the depths of the sea away for the ransomed to pass over?"</u>* Prophetically, Isaiah 27:1 speaks of the Battle of Armageddon, [37] *"In that day the Lord with his sword and great and strong sword shall punish leviathan the piercing serpent, even leviathan that crooked serpent; and he shall slay the dragon that is in the sea."*

(Rahab – Symbolic of Egypt)

Like the Egyptians who worshipped many false gods, Rahab worshipped Baal, Asherah, the moon god, the host of heaven, other false gods, and graven images. In spite of her sin as a whore, she sacrificed to the gods. How ridiculous! Basically, she went from one whore house into another whore house to worship! God disliked her false worship as He despised [38] the Egyptians who worshiped false gods and graven images. God issued a command to His chosen people against graven images, *"Take ye therefore good heed unto yourselves; for ye saw no manner of similitude on the day that the Lord spake unto you in Horeb out of the midst of the fire: Lest ye correct yourselves, and make you a graven image, the similitude of any figure, the likeness of male or female, The likeness of any beast that is on the earth, the likeness of winged fowl that flieth in the air, The likeness of any thing that creepeth on the ground, the likeness of any fish that is in the waters beneath the earth: And lest thou lift up thine eyes unto heaven, and when thou seest the sun, and the moon, and the stars, even all the host of heaven, shouldest be driven to worship them, and serve them, which the Lord thy God hath divided unto all nations under the whole heaven."* (Deuteronomy 4:15-19)

---

[37]   That day refers to the tribulation and the Millennium (1,000 years reign of Christ on earth Revelation 20:1-10)

[38]   Joseph (Jacob's son) despised Egypt so much that he gave a commandment to the children of Israel to carry his bones up out of Egypt. Joseph was embalmed in Egypt and put into coffin. (Genesis 50:22-26)

In Romans 2:23-32, Apostle Paul states, ***"Professing themselves to be wise,*** ***they became fools and changed the glory of the uncorruptible God into an image*** ***made like to corruptible man, and to birds, and fourfooted beasts, and creeping*** ***things.*** *Wherefore, God also gave them up to uncleanness through the lusts* *of their own hearts, to dishonor their own bodies between themselves. Who* *changed the truth of God into a lie, and worshipped and served the creature* *more than the Creator, who blessed forever. For this cause God gave them* *up unto vile affections; or even their women did change the natural use into* *that which is against nature: And likewise also the men, leaving the natural* *use of the woman, burned in their lust one toward another; men with men* *working that which is unseemly, and receiving in themselves that recompense* *of their error which was meet. And even as they did not like to retain God in* *their knowledge, God gave them over to a reprobate mind, to do those things,* *which are not convenient; Being filled with all unrighteousness, fornication,* *wickedness, covetousness, maliciousness; full of envy, murder, debate, deceit,* *malignity; whisperers, backbiters, haters of God, despiteful, proud, boasters,* *inventors of evil things, disobedient to parents, without understanding, covenant* *breakers, without natural affection, implacable, unmerciful: Who knowing* *the judgment of God, that they which commit such things are worthy of death,* *not only do the same, but have pleasure in them that do them. Therefore thou* *art inexcusable, O man..."*

Rahab was not the only one to mimic the Egyptians. Most likely, God was disgusted with *his friend* (Abraham) for going down into Egypt (considering their vile wickedness). During the famine, Abraham did not trust in God to supply all of his needs. Also, Abraham did not petition the Lord for advice for permission to go into Egypt. Just after God called Abraham out of Ur, He directed Abraham to Canaan (the Promised Land). Shortly, there was a famine in land of Canaan and Abraham panicked, ***"And Abram went down into Egypt to sojourn there for*** ***the famine was grievous in the land..."*** (Genesis 12:10-13) In Egypt, Abraham enticed his wife to back-up his misrepresentation (lie) that she was not his wife but rather his sister. Since, Sarah was a beautiful woman, Abraham was afraid that the Egyptians would kill him for her. And rightly so, Pharaoh took Sarah into his household. However, God plagued Pharaoh and his house with great plagues because of Sarah. In spite of Abraham stupidity, God still protected Abraham and his wife. BUT, God condemned Abraham's descendants to four hundred years of Egyptian affliction and servitude. And then, God brought His people out-of-bondage with a mighty hand and drowned Pharaoh and his men in the Red Sea.

Poetically, Egypt (THE HARLOT, like RAHAB the Harlot) was broken into pieces, *"O Lord God of hosts, who is a strong Lord like unto thee? Thou rulest the raging of the sea when the waves there of arise, thou stillest them. Thou has broken Rahab in pieces, as one that is slain; thou has scattered thine enemies with thy strong arm."* (Psalms 87:4)

The Egyptians were descendants of Ham (Noah's son). (Genesis 10:6) Unfortunately, the Egyptians worshipped an accumulation of many false gods: Horus (the sun-god); Osiris (the god of the Nile); the moon god; a god of Memphis; Amon (local-god at Thebes); Re (sun-god at Heliopolis); Amon-Re (Amon received a promotion to Re's status and the names became compounded); Aton (the universal god); and others. Also, The Egyptians worshipped animals (such as the cow, cat, bull, jackal, crocodile) and they put these distinctive animal heads on top of human bodies.

Caption: Egyptian hieroglyphics.

Furthermore, God admonished His people for sojourning to Egypt, *"For thus saith the Lord, <u>Ye have sold yourselves for nought;</u> and ye shall be redeemed without money. <u>For thus saith the Lord God, My people went down aforetime into Egypt to sojourn there;</u> and the Assyrian oppressed them without cause. Now therefore, what have I here, saith the Lord, that my people is taken away for nought? They that rule over them make them to howl, saith the Lord; and my name continually everyday is blasphemed. Therefore my people shall know my name: therefore they shall know in the day that I am he that doth speak: a behold, it is I."* (Isaiah 52:3-6)

The Whore of Babylon

Rahab symbolized the "great whore" in the Book of Revelation. By profession, Rahab was a harlot that makes her a *daughter* of the *Mother of Harlots* and Rahab worshipped false gods and false religions. Nimrod (the son of Cush) was a founder of "false religions" and the "founder of kingdoms" such as *Babylon* (Genesis 10:6) and *Nineveh* (Genesis 10:8-11). Nimrod was a dangerous enemy to God. Nimrod's name means **rebel**. Although he was a mighty hunter, this means nothing! Psalm 52:1-4 states,

"Why boastest thou thyself in mischief, O mighty man? The goodness of God endureth continually. Thy tongue deviseth mischiefs; like a sharp razor, working deceitfully. Thou lovest evil more than good; and lying rather than to speak righteousness. Thou lovest all devouring words, O thou deceitful tongue."

Nimrod was extremely wicked and evil; and this included his queen, Semiramis. They taught men to rebel against God by worshipping objects, the host of heaven, a queen of heaven, a father of heaven; and a son of heaven and these concepts spread throughout the land. As stated earlier, the earth was of one language. Because of their rebellion and production of the tower of Babel, the Lord came down to see, confuse their language, and He scattered them throughout the earth.

Apostle John gives a description of the "great whore" in the Book of Revelation 17:1-5. Also, this description relates to Rahab as well as any harlot.

"Come hither: I will shew unto thee the judgment of the great whore that sitteth upon many waters:

With whom the kings of the earth have committed fornication, and the inhabitants of the earth have been made drunk with the wine of her fornication.

So he carried me away in the spirit into the wilderness: and I saw a woman sit upon a scarlet colored beast, full of names of blasphemy...

<u>*And the woman was arrayed in purple and scarlet color and decked with gold and precious stones and pearls*</u>*, having a golden cup in her hand full of abominations and filthiness of her fornication.*

And upon her forehead was a name written, mystery, Babylon the great, the mother of harlots and abominations of the earth."

The Israelite Spies

"And Joshua the son of Nun sent out of Shittim two men to spy secretly, saying, Go view the land, even Jericho. <u>And they went, and came into an harlot's house, named Rahab, and lodged there</u>." (Joshua 2:1)

So, we find these two *upstanding citizens* of the children of Israel in the *house of a whore*, Rahab. What's up with that? How did they know to knock on Rahab's door? Since, Rahab's house was built into the city's wall did the two spies look up and see Rahab in the window? Perhaps, Rahab was up on the rooftop looking down at the travelers coming into the city's gate! Did she yell out *"Hey you two, who are you, come here?"* One thing for sure, the two spies were men. And as men, they knew <u>exactly</u> where to get a quick course about the city's infrastructure. They went to the house of a whore that told them everything they needed to know. *In fact, they didn't have to go any further than Rahab's house*, that proves she had the <u>www.com</u> on everything in the city of Jericho!

Why didn't Joshua send twelve spies? In the first place, Joshua was extremely confidential about his motives. Perhaps, Joshua remembered the time that Moses commissioned him to spy out the Promised Land with eleven other men. The reports were all negative with the exception of two spies, Caleb and Joshua. Maybe, Joshua wanted to avoid such confusion and controversy so he sent two reliable (unnamed) men. Without fail, the two spies gave *undisputed* reports, ***"Truly the Lord hath delivered into our hands all the land; for even all the inhabitants of the country do faint because of us."*** (Joshua 2:24)

The King's Request

Word got around very quickly in the city Jericho. The king had spies and informers posted throughout the city, ***"And it was told the king of Jericho, saying, behold, there came men in hither to night of the children of Israel to search out all the country. And the king of Jericho sent unto Rahab, saying, bring forth the men that are come to thee, which are entered into thing house: for they be come to search out all the country."*** (Joshua 2:2-3)

Rahab the Protector

Something was happening on the inside to Rahab. The Bible does not say that the harlot or whore hid the two men. Joshua 2:4a, 6 states, ***<u>And the woman took the two men and hid them</u>...she brought them up to the roof of the house, and hid them with the stalks of flax, which she had laid in order upon the roof."*** At that very moment, Rahab was no longer *Rahab the Harlot*, but she was now *"a woman with a compassionate heart."* Some people like to say that once a whore, always a whore, but this is not true when God is working on the heart. God had a specific purpose for Rahab's life. If the Lord opened the mouth of a "female" donkey that talked to Balaam, He could use a "female" prostitute to help His people. Rahab's heart was in the process of "being molded" by the Lord.

When the king's men came to *Rahab's Inn*, she lied to protect the two strangers and redirected the king's men by saying, ***"There came men unto me but I wist*** *not whence they were: And it came to pass about the time of shutting of the gate, when it was dark, that the men went out: whither the men went I wot not: pursue after them quickly; for ye shall overtake them."* (Joshua 2:4b-5) So, the king's *"men pursued after them the way to Jordan unto the fords: and as soon as they were gone out, they shut the gate."* (Joshua 2:7)

Rahab's Testimony & Dialogue with the Spies

After Rahab watched the king's gatekeepers shut the gate, she went up to the rooftop of her inn to the spies saying:

"I know that the Lord hath given you the land, and that your terror is fallen upon us, and that all the inhabitants of the land faint because of you.

For we have heard how the Lord dried up the water of the Red Sea for you, when ye came out of Egypt; and what ye did unto the two kings of the Amorites, that were on the other side Jordan, Sihon and Og, whom ye utterly destroyed.

And as soon as we had heard these things, our hearts did melt, neither did there remain any more courage in any man, because of you: for the Lord your God, he is God in heaven above, and in earth beneath.

Now therefore, I pray you, swear unto me by the Lord, since I have shewed you kindness, that ye will also shew kindness unto my father's house, and give me a true token:

And that ye will save alive my father, and my mother, and my brethren, and my sisters, and all that they have, and deliver our lives from death.

And the men answered her, our life for yours, if ye utter not this our business. And it shall be, when the Lord hath given us the land, that we will deal kindly and truly with thee.

Then she let them down by a cord through the window: for her house was upon the town wall, and she dwelt upon the wall.

And she said unto them, Get you to the mountain, lest the pursuers meet you; and hide yourselves there three days, until the pursuers be returned; and afterward may ye go your way.

And the men said unto her, We will be blameless of this thine oath which thou hast made us swear.

Behold, when we come into the land, thou shalt bind this line of scarlet thread in the window which thou didst let us down by: and thou shalt bring thy father, and thy mother, and thy brethren, and all the father's household home unto thee. And it shall be, that whosoever shall go out of the doors of thy house into the street, his blood shall be upon his head, and we will be guiltless: and whosoever shall be with thee in the house, his blood shall be on our head, if any hand be upon him.

And if thou utter this our business, then we will be guitless of thine oath which thou hast made us to swear. And she said, According unto your words, so be it. And she sent them away, and they departed: and she bound the scarlet line in the window.

And they went and came unto the mountain, and abode there three days, until the pursuers were returned: and the pursuers sought them throughout all the way, but found them not. So the two men returned, and descended from the mountain, and passed over, and came to Joshua the son of Nun, and told him all things that befell them;

And they said unto Joshua, Truly the Lord hath delivered into our hands all the land; for even all the inhabitants of the country do faint because of us."
(Joshua 2:8-24)

The Red Sea Ordeal

Rightfully so, Rahab and the inhabitants of Canaan were scared to death of the Lord! In order to prove Himself to the Egyptians and the world, God hardened Pharaoh's heart. After the death of the firstborn, Pharaoh was beaten (and for a short moment), he deviated from his madness to free the Hebrew slaves.

The story, the fame, and the glory of the one true **_Living God_** spread throughout the land, and today, it is still being retold. **_"And Moses stretched out his hand over the sea and the Lord caused the sea to go back by a strong east wind [God blew through His nostrils] all that night and made the sea dry land, and the waters were divided. And the children of Israel went into the midst of the sea upon the dry ground and the waters were a wall unto them on their right hand and on their left...And the Egyptians pursued and went in after them to the midst of the sea, even Pharaoh's horses, his chariots, and his horsemen...And it came to pass that in the morning watch the Lord looked unto the host of the Egyptians, through the pillar of fire and of the cloud, and troubled the host of the Egyptians. And took off their chariot wheels that they drave them heavily: so that the Egyptians said, Let us flee from the face of Israel; for the Lord fighteth for them against the Egyptians. And the Lord said unto Moses, Stretch out thine hand over the sea, that the waters may come again upon the Egyptians, upon their chariots, and upon their horsemen._**

And Moses stretched forth his hand over the sea, and the sea returned to his strength when the morning appeared and the Egyptians fled against it; and the Lord overthrew the Egyptians in the midst of the sea. And the waters returned and covered the chariots, and the horsemen, and all the host of Pharaoh that came into the sea after them; there remained not so much as one of them...Thus the Lord saved Israel that day out of the hand of the Egyptians; and Israel saw the Egyptians dead upon the sea shore. And Israel saw that great work which the Lord did upon the Egyptians: and the people feared the Lord, and believed the Lord, and his servant Moses." (Exodus 14:21-31)

Rahab's Heart

The Lord was already working on Rahab's heart long before the spies came into Jericho. Rahab could not wait to privately speak with the spies. Listen again to her opening statement, ***"I know that the Lord hath given you the land... terror is fallen upon us and all the inhabitants of the land...we heard how the Lord dried up the Red Sea for you when ye came out of Egypt..."*** Although the spies told Rahab that the city was "condemned by God," they really didn't have to say anything! Rahab already knew what terror awaited Jericho and the land of Canaan.

Truly, Rahab's heart was changed and she was saved by her testimony! She admitted to the spies, **"For the Lord your God, he is God in heaven above, and in earth beneath."** (Joshua 2:11) She no longer thought about her filthy *inn, perfumes, clothing, quests, alcohol, money,* or *fortune.* Moreover, Rahab didn't insult the spies with a bribe. Rather, she humbled herself before the spies. She was concerned about *saving herself and the lives* of her mother, father, brothers, sisters, etc. For this reason, she begged and pleaded with the spies to save her household, ***"I pray you, swear unto me by the Lord, since I have shewed you kindness, that ye will also shew kindness unto my father, my mother, my brethren, my sisters, and all that they have, and deliver our lives from death."***

The Pledge

The two Israelite spies had compassion for Rahab and they respected her request. Of course, the spies realized (without Rahab's help), the king's men would seize and execute them. Also, the spies gave Rahab an *ultimatum* and she was under oath *not to* expose their business to anyone. So they made a *conditional contract* with Rahab, **"Our life for yours, if ye utter not this our business...We will be blameless of this thine oath which thou hast made us swear..."** (Joshua 2:14, 17)

The Scarlet Thread

The "scarlet thread" typified the "blood of Christ" [39] and a symbolism of the Lord's Passover. During the children of Israel's bondage in Egypt, the Lord *"passed over"* the blood on the doorposts of His people, but He took the souls of all firstborn (including man and beast) in Egypt. On that great night (and *"Oh What A Night"*), there was no covering without "unblemished blood."

The Lord spoke to Moses and Aaron in the Land of Egypt, ***"This month shall be unto you the beginning of months: it shall be the first month of the year to you. Speak ye unto all the congregation, saying, In the tenth day of this month they shall take to them every man a lamb, according to the house of their fathers, a lamb for an house…Your lamb shall be without blemish…"*** (Exodus 12:1-5) The children of Israel sprinkled the blood of an unblemished lamb on the doorposts, ***"And they shall take of the blood, and strike it on the two side posts and on the upper door post of the houses."*** (Exodus 12:7)

God said, ***"For I will pass through the land of Egypt this night, and will smite all the firstborn in the land of Egypt, both man and beasts: and against all the gods of Egypt I will execute judgment: I am the Lord. And the blood shall be to you for a token upon the houses where ye are: and when I see the blood, I will pass over you, and the plague shall not be upon you to destroy you, when I smite the land of Egypt."*** (Exodus 12:12-13) Furthermore, the children of Israel were told to memorialize that day, ***"And this day shall be unto you for a memorial: and ye shall keep it a feast by an ordinance for ever."*** (Exodus 12:14)

Therefore, *"the scarlet thread"* represented a *"blood covering"* to Rahab and her family. Because of *"the scarlet thread"* hanging outside of the window, God allowed Joshua to "pass over" *Rahab's Inn.* The two spies told Rahab, **"Behold, when we come into the land, thou shalt <u>Bind this line of scarlet thread in the window which thou didst let us down by</u>…*bring thy father, mother, brethren, and all***

---

[39]   The scarlet represented the blood of Jesus Christ shed on the cross for the sins of the world, but the Lamb of God was already slain from before the foundations of the world.

thy father's household home unto thee. Whosoever shall go out of the doors of thy house into the street, his blood shall be upon his head, and we will be guitless: and whosoever shall be with thee in the house, his blood shall be on our head, if any hand be upon him." (Joshua 2:18-19)

Rahab's Inn - Sanctuary

By definition, sanctuary means *"a holy place as a building set aside for worship; a place of refuge or protection; immunity from punishment or the law as by taking refuge in a church or shelter."* **(Webster's NewWorld Dictionary)** Rahab believed in the God of the children of Israel; therefore, her *Inn* became **"sanctuary"** for her and her entire family. In fact, anyone including the hateful king, the wicked priests and priestesses, or the vilest criminal in Jericho could have been spared under Rahab's roof (sanctuary).

God bestowed "grace" upon Rahab and her family. Biblically, "grace" is "unmerited" favor from God. It is something that cannot be bought or earned! God freely gives it to us.

Chapter Ten

Joshua Magnified

On the day that Joshua and the children of Israel crossed over the Jordan River, the Lord magnified Joshua (as He did Moses), *"And the Lord said unto Joshua, This day will I begin to magnify thee in the sight of all Israel, that they may know that, as I was with Moses, so I will be with thee...And Joshua said unto the children of Israel, Come hither, and hear the words of the Lord your God. And Joshua said, Hereby ye shall know that the living God is among you, and that he will without fail drive out from before you the Canaanites, and the Hittites, and the Hivites, and the Perizzites, and the Girgashites, and the Amorites, and the Jebusites."* (Joshua 3:7, 9-10) For example, the Old Testament states the people of Egypt feared Moses, *"The man Moses was very great in the land of Egypt, in the sight of Pharaoh's servants, and in the sight of the people."* (Exodus 11:3)

Jordan River Crossing

This story of the Jordan River crossing is similar to Red Sea crossing that the children of Israel's experienced in Egypt. This crossing of the Jordan River was a spectacular event,

"And it came to pass, when the people removed from their tents, to pass over Jordan, and the priests bearing the ark of the covenant before the people;

And as they that bare the ark were come unto Jordan and the feet of the priests that bare the ark were dipped in the brim of the water, (for Jordan

overfloweth all his banks all the time of harvest). That the waters which came down from above stood and rose up upon an heap very far from the city Adam, that is beside Zaretan; and those that came down toward the sea of the plain, even the salt sea, failed, and were cut off: and the people passed over right against Jericho.

And the priests that bare the ark of the covenant of the Lord stood firm on dry ground in the midst of Jordan, and all the Israelites passed over on dry ground, until all the people were passed clean over Jordan." (Joshua 3:14-17)

The Jordan Memorials

God dried up the waters of the Jordan (as He dried up the Red Sea) for the children of Israel to cross over into the Promised Land. The children of Israel erected two heaps of stones as a memorial.

The Jordan River and the Red Sea crossings were an awesome sight to behold. Over the past years, movies (about the Ten Commandments, the Red Sea, and other Biblical topics) were made for modern men and women to envision such ordeals! Today, should in-process phenomena take place, men would sell tickets to the event and only the rich could afford to purchase them. The FBI would place restrictions on the ground and common areas so that no one without a government clearance could see. Others would capture the miracles [40] taking aerial photographs, movie cameras, video recorders, cameras, and cell phone snapshots to record such events. This does not include painters, artists, writers, newspaper reporters, and the major networks from all over the world that would come to witness such a phenomena. [41] For all of these aforementioned reasons, *God has manifested Himself in a personal way to every individual.* He is not the God of the rich or poor, He is God over all – Jew and Gentile (male and female).

---

[40]   This is in reference to the crossings of the Jordan River Crossing and the Red Sea.

[41]   Is this the way God wants to save us? No way! He does not have to perform miracles for us to believe. Furthermore, the water does not have to stand up ninety stories for me to accept God as God. God is the creator of heaven and earth! That is good enough for me.

Unfortunately, modern technologies and other such devises were not available in ancient times to the children of Israelites. Rather, the crossing of the Jordan River and the Red Sea were recorded in the memory of the minds of the participants and in the minds of the people who lived in the surrounding areas. Although, the inhabitants of Canaan did not witness the Jordan River miracle, they heard about it and the power of the Hebrew's God.

For example, the residents in the land of Canaan were frightened out-of-their minds,

*"**And it came to pass when all the kings of the Amorites, which were on the side of Jordan westward, and all the kings of the Canaanites, which were by the sea, heard that the Lord had dried up the waters of Jordan from before the children of Israel, until we were passed over, that their heart melted, neither was there spirit in them any more, because of the children of Israel.**"* (Joshua 5:1)

Memorial #1

However, the Lord spake to Joshua, *"Take you twelve men out of the people, out of every tribe a man and command ye them saying, Take you hence out of the midst of Jordan, out of the place where the priests' feet stood firm, twelve stones, and ye shall carry them over with you, and leave them in the lodging place, where ye shall lodge this night that this may be a sign among you, that when your children ask their fathers in time to come, saying what mean ye by these stones? Then ye shall answer them, that the waters of Jordan were cut off before the ark of the covenant of the Lord: when it passed over Jordan, the waters of Jordan were cut off, and these stones shall be for a memorial unto the children of Israel forever. And the children of Israel dos o as Joshua commanded and took up twelve stones out of the midst of Jordan, as the Lord spake unto Joshua, according to the number of the tribes of the children of Israel and carried them over with them unto the place where they lodged, and laid them down there. "* (Joshua 4:1-8)

Memorial #2

Somehow, Joshua decided to set up a second memorial to commemorate the Jordan River crossing. It seems that Joshua had compassion for the priests (who were standing and holding the Ark of the Covenant all day in the middle of the Jordan River) and he wanted to put stones in the place where their feet stood.

"And Joshua set up twelve stones in the midst of Jordan in the place where the feet of the priests which bare the ark of the covenant stood: and they are there unto this day.

For the priest which bare the ark stood in the midst of Jordan until every thing was finished that the Lord commanded Joshua to speak unto the people, according to all that Moses commanded Joshua: and the people hasted and passed over.

And it came to pass, when all the people were clean passed over, that the ark of the Lord passed over, and the priests, in the presence of the people."
(Joshua 4:9-13)

Chapter Eleven

On the Other Side

God told Joshua to circumcise the children of Israel to roll away the reproach of Egypt,

"Make thee sharp knives, and circumcise again the children of Israel the second time. And Joshua made him sharp knives, and circumcised the children of Israel at the hill of the foreskins.

And this is the cause why Joshua did circumcise: All the people that came out of Egypt, that were males, even all the men of war, died in the wilderness by the way, after they came out of Egypt.

Now all the people that came out were circumcised: but all the people that were born in the wilderness by the way as they came forth out of Egypt, them they had not circumcised.

For the children of Israel walked forty years in the wilderness, till all the people that were men of war, which came out of Egypt, were consumed, because they obeyed not the voice of the Lord: unto whom the Lord sware that he would not shew them the land, which the Lord sware unto their fathers that he would give us, a land that floweth with milk and honey.

And their children, whom he raised up in their stead, them Joshua circumcised: for they were uncircumcised, because they had not circumcised them by the way.

And their children, whom he raised up in their stead, them Joshua circumcised: for they were uncircumcised, because they had not circumcised them by the way.

And it came to pass, when they had done circumcising all the people, that they abode in their places, that they abode in their place in the camp, till they were whole.

And the Lord said unto Joshua, This day have I rolled away the reproach of Egypt from off you. Wherefore the name of the place is called Gilgal unto this day." (Joshua 5:2-9)

Manna Ceased

After the first Passover in the land of Canaan, the children of Israel ate old corn which they purchased from the people of the land.

"And they did eat of the old corn of the land on the morrow after the Passover, unleavened cake, and parched corn in the selfsame day.

And the manna ceased on the morrow after they had eaten of the old corn of the land; neither had the children of Israel manna any more; but they did eat of the fruit of the land of Canaan that year." (Joshua 5:10-12)

Fall of Jericho

The entire city of Jericho was air tight,   *"Now Jericho was straitly shut up because of the children of Israel: none went out and none came in.*

"And the Lord said unto Joshua, See, I have given into thine hand Jericho, and the king thereof, and the mighty men of valor.

And ye shall compass the city, all ye men of war, and go round about the city once. Thus shalt thou do six days.

Caption: **Joshua and the fall of Jericho.**

And seven priests shall bear before the ark seven trumpets of rams' horns: and the seventh day ye shall compass the city seven times, and the priests shall blow with the trumpets.

And it shall come to pass that when they make a long blasts with the ram's horn, and when ye hear the sound of the trumpet, all the people shall shout with a great shout; and the wall of the city shall fall down flat, and the people shall ascend up every man straight before him.

And Joshua the son of Nun called the priests, and said unto them, Take up the Ark of the Covenant, and let seven priests bear seven trumpets of rams' horns before the ark of the Lord.

And he said unto the people, Pass on, and compass the city, and let him that is armed pass on before the ark of the Lord... (Joshua 6:1-7)

"And it came to pass on the seventh day that they rose early about the dawning of the day, and compassed the city after the same manner seven times: only on that day they compassed the city seven times.

And it came to pass at the seventh time, when the priests blew with the trumpets, Joshua said unto the people, Shout: for the Lord hath given you the city." (Joshua 6:15-16)

"So the people shouted when the priests blew with the trumpets: and it came to pass, when the people heard the sound of the trumpet, and the people shouted with a great shout, the wall fell down flat, so that the people went up into the city, every man straight before him, and they took the city.

And they utterly destroyed all that was in the city, both man and woman, young and old, and ox, and sheep, and ass, with the edge of the sword.

But Joshua said unto the two men that had spied out the country, Go into to harlot's house and bring out thence the woman, and all that she hath as ye sware unto her." (Joshua 17-22)

Through divine guidance and intervention, Joshua and the children of Israel destroyed the wall and burned the city with fire but they saved *one* particular family. After the defeat, Joshua launched a prophecy against Jericho and the person endeavoring to rebuild the city and this prophecy remained in effect for decades. Joshua 6:26 states, *"And Joshua adjured them at that time, saying, Cursed be the man before the Lord, that riseth up and buildeth this city Jericho: he shall lay the foundation thereof in his first born, and in his youngest son shall he set up the gates of it. So the Lord was with Joshua; and his fame was noised throughout all the country."*

During the reign of king Ahab of Israel (approximately four hundred years later), Joshua's curse was fulfilled. First Kings 16:34 states, *"In his days [Ahab's command] did Hiel the Bethelite build Jericho: he laid the foundation thereof in Abiram his firstborn, and set up the gates thereof in his youngest son Segub, according to the word of the Lord, which he spake by Joshua the son of Nun."*

Chapter Twelve

Salvation Comes to Rahab

Hallelujah! Inside of *Rahab's Inn*, there was fear and trembling. What if the spies forgot to tell the Israelite men of war about the "scarlet cord" hanging outside of the window? What if the scarlet cord broke and the men of war assumed that *Rahab's Inn* was next in line for attack? Rahab's mother and sisters (and sister-in-laws and all the children) sobbed relentlessly, because they heard the cries of help, slaughter, and destruction in the streets of Jericho. It was frightening and confusing! They knew these people. Towering over the cries of the victims, they heard the *sounds of victory* and *jubilee* from the children of Israel. Paradoxically, the children of Israel were their enemies and their rescuers.

Rahab remained calm because she trusted in the Lord God of Israel. As she got closer to God, Rahab's heart was being circumcised! Because of her penitent heart, salvation came to Rahab and her family. Rahab consoled the members of her family! Probably, Rahab spoke the following words to her parents and family, *"I have shown kindness to the Israelite spies by saving their lives, and now, they will spare all of our lives. Do not leave this place or run out into the street. My house was a house of sin but it is now sanctuary to you and to all that are within these walls…"*

After the fighting ended, Joshua told the two *young* spies, ***"Go into the harlot's house and bring out thence the woman, and all that she hath, as ye sware unto her."*** Notice, Joshua said, "Go into the harlot's house." But, then he said, **"Bring out the woman!"** At this point, ***Rahab was saved! Remember,*** Joshua means **"God is salvation."** In the New Testament, Acts 4:12 states, ***"Neither is there salvation in any other for there is none other name under heaven among men***

98

whereby we must be saved." Joshua was just standing in the for the Lord! Prior to this, Rahab had already confessed belief in the Lord God of Israel.

And the young men that were spies went in and brought out Rahab, and her father, and her mother, and her brethren, and all that she had; and they brought out all her kindred, and left them without the camp of Israel.

And they burnt the city with fire, and all that was therein: only the silver, and the gold, and the vessels of brass and of iron, they put into the treasury of the house of the Lord." (Joshua 6:22-24)

Similarities - Rahab & Lot's Dilemmas

On a much smaller scale, the destruction of Jericho was similar to the *destruction of Sodom, Gomorrah, and the cities of the plains.* All of the cities were **damned**! The *two spies* in Rahab's story are symbolic of the *two angels* in Lot's story. Rahab and her family were told to stay within the walls of her house; *but the two angels told Lot and his family to flee for their lives.* After the battle was over, the spies came back for Rahab (and her family) to lead them out of the city. *Likewise the angels led Lot (by the hand) out-of-the city before the destruction of the cities.* As long as Rahab remained in her house, the house itself was under protection. Afterward, *Rahab's Inn* perished in the fire of the damned as *Lot's house perished in God's rain of fire and brimstone on the accursed cities of the plains.* Rahab's end was victorious and she married into a prominent family of Judah. Unlike Rahab, *Lot had a shameful end! His wife was destroyed for disobedience (her flesh and blood was turned into a pillar of salt) and Lot's daughters committed incest with him.*

Like Rahab and her family, *Lot and his family were warned of the impending destruction to the cities.* Rahab shared the impending danger with only her family members and petitioned them to avoid the upcoming disaster. *Lot shared the impending danger with his family members and his two son-in-laws. Unfortunately, Lot's two son-in-laws mocked him. Perhaps, they thought Lot had too much wine, or perhaps, they were too deep in sin.* Rahab's family humbled themselves and obeyed her advice. Rahab heeded to the voices of mercy (the two spies) and hastily she brought her family into the sanctuary.

In contrast, Lot was disobedient and he lingered at the promises of mercy. At first, Lot <u>refused</u> to go into the mountains (the chosen sanctuary as instructed by the angels) saying, "I cannot escape to the mountain lest some evil take me and I die..." (Genesis 19:19) *Astonishingly, Lot selected a city of refuge for himself and his family to hide in, Zoar (means "a small insignificant city"). Shortly after Lot's arrival in Zoar, he flew out of the city (like a speeding bullet) because it was filled with the same sin as Sodom and Gomorrah. Honestly, Lot set-up himself for failure, "he had it his way!" Frankly, Zoar was on the hit list to be destroyed, but the angels spared it just because Lot wanted sanctuary in it! Because of God's mercy to Lot, we have an extraordinary break in policy or an exception to the rule. God extended His mercy to an entire sin-filled city for the sake of four people, Lot, his wife, and their two daughters.* Remember, Abraham asked God not to destroy the cities of the plain for five righteous souls!

Many times, king David spoke and wrote about the mercies of God. In II Samuel 24, king David committed his last sin of numbering Israel (God said that the children of Israel would be without numbering as the stars in heaven and the dust of the earth). For David's mistake, God sent Gad (the seer) to offer David three choices of punishment. However, God's act of mercy was recorded as follows, ***"And David said unto Gad I am in a great strait: <u>let us fall now into the hand of the Lord; for his mercies are great; and let me not fall into the hand of man</u>. So the Lord sent a pestilence upon Israel from the morning even to the time appointed: <u>and there died of the people from Dan even to Beersheba seventy thousand men. And when the angel stretched out his hand upon Jerusalem to destroy it, the Lord repented him of the evil, and said to the angel that destroyed the people, It is enough: stay now thine hand.</u> And the angel of the Lord was by the threshing place of Araunah the Jebusite."*** (II Samuel 24:14-16) Like Lot who spoke to the two angels, king David saw the angel of the Lord, and he said, ***"I have done wickedly but these sheep what have they done? Let thine hand, I pray thee, be against me, and against my father's house."*** (II Samuel 24:17)

The Sodom and Gomorrah Ordeal

According to Genesis Chapter 19, Lot was at leisure on the day of the divine visitors came to Sodom,

*"**And there came two angels to Sodom at even; and Lot sat in the gate of Sodom: and Lot seeing them rose up to meet them; and he bowed himself with his face toward the ground;***

And he said, Behold now, my lord, turn in, I pray you, into your servant's house, and tarry all night, and wash your feet, and ye shall rise up early, and go on your ways. And they said, Nay; but we will abide in the street all night.*

And he pressed upon them greatly; and they turned in unto him, and entered into his house; and he made them a fast, and did bake unleavened bread, and they did eat.

But before they lay down, the men of the city even the men of Sodom, compassed the house round, both old and young, all the people from every quarter:

And they called unto Lot and said unto him, Where are the men which came in to thee this night? Bring them out unto us, that we may know them.

And Lot went out at the door unto them, and shut the door after him,

And said, I pray you, brethren, do not so wickedly. Behold now, I have two daughters which have not known man; let me, I pray you, bring them out unto you, and do ye to them as is good in your eyes: only unto these men do nothing; for therefore came they under the shadow of my roof.

And they [men of the city] said, Stand back. And they said again, This one fellow came in to sojourn, and he will needs be a judge: now will we deal worse

with thee, than with them. And they pressed sore upon the man, even Lot, and came near to break the door.

But the men [angels] put forth their hand, and pulled Lot into the house to them, and shut the door.

And they smote the men that were at the door of the house with blindness, both small and great: so that they wearied themselves to find the door...

And the men [angels] said unto Lot, Hast thou here any besides? Sons in law, and they sons, and thy daughters, and whatsoever thou hast in the city, bring them out of this place:

For we will destroy this place, because the cry of them is waxen great before the face of the Lord; and the Lord hath sent us to destroy it .And Lot went out, and spake unto his sons in law, which married his daughters, and said, Up, get you out of this place; for the Lord will destroy this city.

But he seemed as one that mocked unto his sons in law. And when the morning arose, then the [two] Angels hastened Lot saying, Arise take thy wife and thy two daughters which are here; least thou be consumed in the iniquity of the city. <u>And while he lingered, the men [angels] laid hold upon his hand, and upon the hand of his wife, and upon the hand of his two daughters: the Lord being merciful unto him: and thy brought him forth, and set him without the city.</u>" (Genesis 19:1-16)

"And it came to pass, when they [angels] had brought them [Lot & his family] abroad, that he said, Escape for thy life; look not behind thee, neither stay thou in all the plain; escape to the mountain lest thou be consumed.

And Lot said unto them, <u>Oh, not so, my Lord;</u>

Behold now, thy servant hath found grace in thy sight, and thou hast magnified thy mercy, which thou hast shewed unto me in saving my life; and I cannot escape to the mountain, lest some evil take me, and I die:

Behold now, this city is near to flee unto, and it is a little one: Oh, let me escape thither, (is it not a little one?) and my soul shall live.

And he said unto him, See I have accepted thee concerning this thing also, that I will not overthrow this city, for the which thou hast spoken.

Haste thee, escape thither; for I cannot do any thing till thou be come thither. Therefore the name of the city was called Zoar.

The sun was risen upon the earth when Lot entered into Zoar.

Then the Lord rained upon Sodom and upon Gomorrah brimstone and fire from the Lord out of heaven;

And he overthrew those cities, and all the plain, and all the inhabitants of the cities, and that which grew upon the ground.

But Lot's wife looked back from behind him, and she became a pillar of salt." (Genesis 19:17-26)

"*And Lot went up out of Zoar, and dwelt in the mountain, and his two daughters with him; for he feared to dwell in Zoar: and he dwelt in a cave, he and his two daughters.*" (Genesis 19:40)

Comparison of Rahab and Gomer

There was another whore named, Gomer (means *"completion"*). God told Hosea (means *"deliverer"*) the son of Beeri and a minor prophet to marry Gomer. Symbolically, Gomer represented the children of Israel and Hosea's love for his wife represented God's love for His people. God told Hosea to marry Gomer (the daughter of Diblaim) a wife of whoredoms (plural). Like Gomer, Rahab was a whore, but God had a destiny for Rahab's life just as He did for Gomer's life. Eventually, Rahab *the ex-harlot* would marry into an eminent family just as Hosea (the minor prophet) married Gomer.

Gomer had three children for Hosea and the names of these children were symbolic of the children of Israel: (1) *a son, Jezreel, means* **"I will avenge the blood of Jezreel upon the house of Jehu;"** (2) *a daughter, Lo-ruhamah, means* **"I will no more have mercy upon the house of Israel; but I will utterly take them away";** and (3) *another son, Lo-ammi, means* **"For ye are not my people, and I will not be your God."** (Hosea 1:1-8) Rahab was destined to be important in the genealogy of Israel.

Like the children of Israel (who left God), Hosea's wife left him for her former lovers and God said, <u>***"Hear the word of the Lord, ye children of Israel: for the Lord hath a controversy with the inhabitants of the land, because there is no truth nor mercy, nor knowledge of God in the land. By swearing, and lying, and killing, and stealing, and committing adultery, they break out, and blood toucheth blood...***"</u> (Hosea 4:1-2)

"My people are destroyed for lack of knowledge: because thou has rejected knowledge, I will also reject thee, that thou shalt be no priest to me, seeing thou hast forgotten the law of thy God. I will also forget thy children. As they increased, so they sinned against me: therefore will I change their glory into shame. They eat up the sin of my people, and they set their heart on their iniquity.

My people ask counsel of their stocks, and their staff declareth unto them: for the spirit of whoredoms hath caused them to err, and they have gone a whoring from under their God.

They sacrifice upon the tops of the mountains, and burn incense upon the hills, under oaks and poplars and elms, because the shadow there is good:

therefore your daughters shall commit whoredom, and your spouses shall commit adultery." (Hosea 4:6-13)

In time, God (who is full of mercy and compassion) will forgive His people and they shall be called Ammi (my people). Of course, this is futuristic. However, God told Hosea to go and get his wife, Gomer, *"Go yet, love a woman beloved of her friend, yet an adulteress, according to the love of the Lord toward the children of Israel, who look to other gods, and love flagons of wine. So I bought her to me for fifteen pieces of silver and for a homer of barley, and a half homer of barley.* (Hosea 3:1-2) Judas Iscariot (one of the twelve disciples of Jesus and the treasurer), betrayed our Lord and Savor for fifteen pieces of silver. (Matthew 26:6-13; Mark 14:10-11; Luke 22:3-6) Twice, Gomer left her husband and children to play the whore and each time Hosea redeemed her. Perhaps for thirty years, Rahab played a harlot, *but one day*, God redeemed her from the life of sin!

Hosea told Gomer, *"<u>Thou shalt not play the harlot and thou shalt not be for another man: so will I also be for thee.</u> For the children of Israel shall abide many days without a king, and without a prince, and without a sacrifice, and without an image, and without an ephod, and without teraphim. Afterward, shall the children of Israel return and seek the Lord their God, and David their king; and shall fear the Lord and his goodness in the latter days."* (Hosea 3:1-5)

Princess Rahab - (Mrs. Salmon of Judah)

As stated earlier, the two spies rescued Rahab and her family from Jericho; but they *"left them outside of the camp of Israel."* (Joshua 6:24) During their time outside of the camp, the family underwent ceremonial cleansing of defilements: (1) the males were circumcised to roll away the reproach of Jericho (the same as Joshua circumcised all the males born in the wilderness even the men of war to roll away the reproach of Egypt); and (2) Rahab and her entire family were treated like lepers, *"All the days wherein the plague shall be in him he shall be defiled: he is unclean; he shall dwell alone; without the camp shall his habitation be... And the priest shall go forth out of the camp and shall look and behold if the plaque of leprosy be healed in the leper...*" (Leviticus 13:46; 14:3) Next, the priest made a sacrifice and performed other rituals according to the law of leprosy. After cleansing, the leper was brought back into the camp. This happened to Miriam (Moses' sister) who was struck with leprosy for rebelling against Moses' marriage to an Ethiopian woman. Moses prayed to the Lord to stop the plague and Miriam was shut outside of the camp for seven days. Furthermore, the children of Israel did not journey until Miriam's healing. (Numbers 12:1-15)

After a period of *cleansing and time outside of the camp*, Rahab's family was grafted into the body of Israel. She was a heroine and admired by all of the children of Israel. Her past was forgiven! Also, there was no record of anyone talking about her pagan parents and family members. More importantly, there was no mention of Rahab's relatives stealing, cheating, or breaking the Law of Moses. They blended in perfectly with their new hosts. Truly, Rahab and her family were accepted.

There was a young prince named, Salma (a.k.a. Salmon) that fell madly in-love with Rahab. Prince Salmon was from the tribe of Judah and his father's name was Nahshon (means *"diviner"*) the brother-in-law to Aaron the Priest. Nahshon's sister (Elisheba) was married to Aaron (Moses' brother). Nahshon and Elisheba's father was Amminadab, captain of the Hebrew host (Numbers 2:3). ***"And Nahshon begat Salma, and Salma begat Boaz, And Boaz begat Obed, and Obed began Jesse... [begat David]"*** (I Chronicles 2:11-12)

New Testament Genealogy (Abraham to Christ)

"In the Book of Matthew, the book of generation of Jesus Christ, the son of David, the son of Abraham,

"Abraham begat Isaac; and Isaac begat Jacob; and Jacob begat Judas [Judah] and his brethren; And Judas begat Phares and Zara of Thamar; and Phares begat Esrom; and Esrom begat Aram;

And Aram begat Aminadab [Amminadab] begat Naason [Nahshon], and Naasson begat Salmon;

And Salmon begat Booz [Boaz] of Rachab [Rahab]; and Booz begat Obed of Ruth; and Obed begat Jesse;

And Jesse begat David the King, and David the king begat Abia; and Abia begat Asa;

And Asa begat Josaphat; and Josaphat begat Joram; and Joram begat Ozias;

And Ozias begat Joatham; and Joatham begat Achaz; and Achaz begat Ezekias;

And Ezekias begat Manasses; and Manasses begat Amon; and Amon begat Josias;

And Josias begat Jechonias and his brethren, about the time they were carried away to Babylon:

And after they were brought to Babylon, Jechonias begat Salathiel; and Salathiel begat Zorobabel;

And Zorobabel begat Abiud; and Abiud begat Eliakim; and Eliakim begat Azor;

And Azor begat Sadoc; and Sadoc begat Achim; and Achim begat Eliud;

And Eliud begat Eleazar; and Eleazar begat Matthan; and Matthan begat Jacob;

And Jacob begat Joseph the husband of Mary,[42] *of whom was born Jesus, who is called Christ.*

So all of the generations from Abraham to David are fourteen generations, and from David unto the carrying away into Babylon are fourteen generations; and from the carrying away into Babylon unto Christ are fourteen generations." (Matthew 1:1-17)

---

[42] *"Behold a virgin shall be with child, and shall bring forth a son, and they shall call his name Emmanuel, which being interpreted is, God with us."* (Matthew 1:23)

Chapter Thirteen

Hall of Faith

"_Now faith is the substance of things hoped for, the evidence of things not seen_. For by it the elders obtained a good report.

Through faith we understand that the worlds were framed by the word of God, so that things which are seen were not made of things which do appear.

By faith, Abel offered unto God a more excellent sacrifice than Cain, by which he obtained witness that he was righteous, God testifying of his gifts: and by it he being dead yet speaketh.

By faith, Enoch was translated that he should not see death; and was not found, because God had translated him: for before his translation he had this testimony,[43] that he pleased God.

But without faith, it is impossible to please him: for he that cometh to God must believe that he is, and that he is a rewarder of them that diligently seek him.

By faith, Noah, being warned of God of things not seen as yet, moved with fear, prepared an ark to the saving of his house; by the which he condemned the world, and became heir of the righteousness which is by faith.

---

43   What is your testimony?

By faith, Abraham, when he was called to go out into a place which he should after receive for an inheritance, obeyed; and he went out, not knowing whither he went.

By faith, he sojourned in the land of promise, as in a strange country, dwelling in tabernacles with Isaac and Jacob, the heirs with him of the same promise:

For he looked for a city which hath foundations, whose builder and maker is God.

Through faith, Sarah herself received strength to conceive seed, and was delivered of a child when she was past age, because she judged him faithful who had promised.

Therefore sprang there even of one, and him as good as dead, so many as the stars of the sky in multitude, and as the sand which is by the sea shore innumerable.

These all died in faith, not having received the promises, but having seen them afar off, and were persuaded of them, and embraced them, and confessed that they were strangers and pilgrims on the earth.

For they that say such things declare plainly that they seek a country.

And truly, if they had been mindful of that country from whence they came out, they might have had opportunity to have returned.

But now they desire a better country, that is, an heavenly: wherefore God is not ashamed to be called their God: for he hath prepared for them a city.

By faith, Abraham when he was tried offered up Isaac: and he that had received the promises offered up his only begotten son,

Of whom it was said, That in Isaac shall thy seed be called:

Accounting that God was able to raise him up, even from the dead; from whence also he received him a figure.

By faith, Isaac blessed Jacob and Esau concerning things to come.

By faith, Jacob when he was a dying, blessed both the sons of Joseph; and worshipped, leaning upon the top of his staff.

By faith, Joseph, when he died, made mention of the departing of the children of Israel; and gave commandment concerning his bones.

By faith, Moses, when he was born, was hid three months of his parents, because they saw he was a proper child; and they were not afraid of the king's commandment.

By faith, Moses when he was come to years, refused to be called son of Pharaoh's daughter;

Choosing rather to suffer affliction with the people of God, than to enjoy the pleasure of sin for a season;

Esteeming the reproach of Christ greater riches than the treasures in Egypt: for he had respect unto the recompence of the reward.

By faith, he forsook Egypt not fearing the wrath of the king: for he endured, as seeing him who is invisible.

Through faith, he kept the Passover, and the sprinkling of blood, lest he that destroyed the firstborn should touch them.

By faith they passed through the Red Sea as by dry land: which the Egyptians assaying to do were drowned.

By faith the walls of Jericho fell down, after they were compassed about seven days.

> *__By faith the harlot, Rahab, perished not with them that believed not, when she had received the spies with peace.__*
>
> *And what shall I say more?"*

Apostle Paul   (Hebrews 11:1-32)

Words for the Reader

It is true - Rahab lived a sinful life as a harlot, but God saved her, her family, and she became an ancestor to JESUS CHRIST! **Yes, Rahab is in the Hall of Fame, the Book of Hebrews 11:31.** *People like to throw stones at sinners, especially whores. But, what about the "johns?" I have a word of caution to those who feel this way.* **Regardless of its size, <u>Sin is Sin</u>**.

You may be in one of the following categories: attend church every Sunday *and through the week; teach Bible classes; sing in the choir; pay tithes on a regular basis; give extra offerings; help paint the church; clean the church; participate in plays at the church or the community; mow the lawn; wash the car; walk the dog; paint the house; go to work; help feed the poor; donate funds to various charity organizations; help needy neighbors/others; drive non-family members to the doctor/hospital; clean the carpet; visit ailing relatives/friends at the rest home; and so-on.* **If there is any type of sin in your life, all the good you are doing will not save you!**

You may be in one of the following categories: dating multiple girlfriends/ boyfriends at the same time *but keeping it real;* avoid hurting feelings *by telling little white lies;* loaning money to others *but expecting favors;* living a double life *but within your rights;* faithfully married *but occasionally date others;* hanging out *while buying drinks for others;* telling a few little dirty jokes *while quoting Bible Scriptures; searching the internet for repair shops while dabbing into pornography sites;* admitting mistakes *but can't stop sinning; justifying your mistakes by bringing flowers and gifts; embarrassed because the spouse is fat but you're bald headed; take the spouse to dinner but hold your head down; can't think of anything nice to say to the spouse but you talk on the cell phone to others in code; take out the family while desiring to be some where else; and so-on.*

If you have not repented of your sin (no matter what the sin may be), you are out of out-of-fellowship with God. You cannot fight your battle alone, and you need the Lord. Look at Rahab's life. Truly, it was horrible but GOD TURNED HER LIFE AROUND. IT DOES NOT MATTER WHO OR WHAT YOU ARE… GOD LOVES YOU AND HE WILL FORGIVE YOU!

Come back to Jesus! Repent of your sin! Everyone makes mistakes but do not keep on making them. After a certain period of time, the Lord will call you on the carpet. What excuse can you give to Jesus? He nailed every excuse to the cross! There is no escape from Him. I dare you to TRY GOD!